HOME ICE ADVANTAGE

HOME ICE ADVANTAGE

a novel

TOM EARLE

Harper*Trophy*Canada™
An imprint of HarperCollins*PublishersLtd*

J PB Earle
445
January 19 2017
C.1

Home Ice Advantage
Copyright © 2013 by Tom Earle.
All rights reserved.

Published by Harper*Trophy*Canada™, an imprint of HarperCollins Publishers Ltd

First published by Harper*Trophy*Canada™ in an original trade paperback edition: 2013
This trade paperback edition: 2016

This is a work of fiction. While the story is set against the actual backdrop of North
American hockey, all people and events are entirely imaginary.

Harper*Trophy*Canada™ is a trademark of HarperCollins Publishers.

HarperCollins books may be purchased for educational, business,
or sales promotional use through our Special Markets Department.

HarperCollins Publishers Ltd
2 Bloor Street East, 20th Floor
Toronto, Ontario, Canada
M4W 1A8

www.harpercollins.ca

Library and Archives Canada Cataloguing in Publication is available upon request

ISBN 978-1-44340-905-6

Printed and bound in the United States of America
RRD 9 8 7 6 5 4 3 2 1

For Lindsay, Nick, and Lucas

PART ONE

CHAPTER ONE

The closet door creaked slightly when I pulled on the handle. I held my breath for a moment, listening, before reaching in for my winter jacket. I slipped it on, then knelt down to pull on my boots. My hands were shaking and I had difficulty with the laces. Maybe this wasn't such a good idea. I could head back to bed, and tomorrow morning we could all pretend that everything was fine. I was still hesitating when I stood up and caught my reflection in the large mirror beside the closet. My left eye was missing, hidden under a swollen welt covering most of that side of my face. A mixture of rage, anger, and self-pity surged through me as I opened the front door and slipped out into the cold night air.

I scurried down the front walk, turned left on the sidewalk, and broke into a dead run. The sound of my footsteps echoed off the fronts of our neighbours' houses. As I rounded the corner onto Sheppard Avenue, I could see the bright, white sign illuminating the entrance to the subway. I smiled to myself and quickened my pace.

CHAPTER TWO

Three months earlier . . .

As I skated onto the ice, I glanced up at the game clock: 2:53 to go in the second period. Beautiful—we were already down three nothing to the Toronto Eagles, the best team in the league, and they were about to start a five-on-three power play. This game was one shot away from turning into a "laugher."

I gotta win the draw, I told myself as I got ready to take the faceoff. *It's our only hope to kill some time before these jokers score another one on us.*

The ref dropped the puck and I fought the Toronto centreman for possession. Just as I was gaining control of it, a Toronto winger darted into the faceoff circle, grabbed the puck, and passed it back to one of his defencemen.

No! I forced my way past the centreman and hustled out to challenge their defenceman. As I skated toward him, I waved my stick back and forth and tried to take away his passing lanes. I didn't want him sending the puck to one of his forwards. If I could force him to shoot from the point, maybe our goalie would have a better chance of making the save. I stopped about a metre in front of him and continued to wave my stick back and forth like a madman. If he was going to shoot, he would have to put one right through me. I hate blocking shots—it just flat out hurts—but when you're down by three goals you do what you have to do. Suddenly, he turned and passed the puck across to his defence partner.

Oh man! I was so busy worrying about his forwards that I forgot about his defence partner. I skated as hard as I could to take away the shot, but I was too late. He had a wide-open lane to our net and all I could do was watch as he wound up for a slapshot. But instead of shooting, he faked and pivoted back toward his partner. *These guys wanna make me look stupid before they score,* I thought. As the defenceman made his pretty little slap pass back across the blue line, I lunged out with my stick. Miraculously, the puck hit the blade of my stick and bounced out into the neutral zone.

Go, go go! I commanded myself. I took off up the ice with the two Toronto defencemen converging on me from either side. I was still just thinking about getting the puck and knocking it down into their zone to kill more penalty time, but when I got to the puck I was a stride ahead of both of them. I grabbed it and accelerated toward their goaltender.

When I hit Toronto's blue line, I looked up to see their goalie coming way out of his net to challenge me.

You want me to deke, huh? I thought. He was out so far that there really was no point trying to shoot; I couldn't even see the net.

I faked with my head to my backhand, and then slid the puck to my forehand. As the goalie moved to follow me, I pulled the puck to my backhand and flicked a little saucer shot between his legs. As I flew past him, I could see that the puck was already in the back of the net.

I could hear our fans roar as I circled into the corner, raised my stick, and grinned. A two-man-short-goal against the Toronto Eagles—not too shabby.

The goal seemed to stun the Eagles, and not only did we kill off the rest of the penalty, but we started taking the game to them. Early in the third period, we broke out of our own end. I peeled into the corner and dashed up the left wall. One of our defencemen passed to me, and I blew around the Eagles' defence, cutting hard to the net. The goalie dove at me and tried to poke-check the puck away, but I backhanded it up and over him to cut the Eagles' lead to one goal.

The game stayed that way until late in the third period when I found myself sitting on the bench, gasping for breath. I took a quick gulp of water and tried not to watch the clock as it ticked agonizingly toward the end of the game. I willed my teammates to get the puck into the Eagles' zone and tie the game. At the very least, I hoped that they would force a faceoff, so my line could come out on a fresh line change. As my teammates gained the red line then slammed the puck into the attacking zone, I felt a hand on my shoulder.

"Get ready to go for Freddie," Coach Madigan ordered. "If we don't get a faceoff, I'll have to pull him."

"Okay, Coach."

He patted my shoulder. "You've already beat this kid twice, Jakey. A hat trick would be a nice way to tie the game."

I nodded and tried to calm down. Madigan always seemed to know how to get me to relax under pressure. We could be in the final of the All Ontario's, and he wouldn't get the least bit ruffled. I stood and moved to the gate, where Mr. Whitney, our assistant coach, waited nervously to open it for me. He tried to smile, but he looked like he was on the verge of being sick to his stomach.

"Tie this thing up, will ya, Jakey?" he asked hopefully.

"I'll do my—"

"Jake!" Madigan yelled down the bench. "I'm pulling Freddie." He turned and waved frantically at our goaltender. "Freddie! Come on!"

Freddie bolted for the defencemen's gate. When he was almost there, Coach Whitney opened the forwards' door and yelled, "Go get 'em, Jake!"

I charged out the gate toward the Eagles' zone and arrived just as my opponents were working the puck up the boards. If they cleared the zone, it would all but end the game because we wouldn't have time to regroup and launch a final assault on their net.

The puck popped loose and bounced toward the Eagles' right winger. I flattened him with a solid bodycheck before he could clear it out. The clock in my head told me that we only had a few seconds left in the game. I grabbed the loose puck, wound up, and released a wicked slapshot from just above the left faceoff circle. The shot beat the goalie high to the glove side, and the puck rang loudly off the crossbar. It ricocheted high up into the protective mesh behind the net just as the horn blared to signal the end of the game.

I watched helplessly as the Eagles whooped it up, congratulating their goaltender on a hard-fought victory. My shoulders sagged and my head dropped.

My teammate Joey Winslow skated by and whacked me on the shin pads with his stick. "Almost, Jake." He smiled. "It was a hell of a shot, buddy. Goalie never even moved."

I skated slowly back to our end of the ice to give Freddie a half-hearted tap on the pads and pat on the head.

We filed quietly into the locker room, removed our helmets, and mouth and neck guards, and waited for Coach Madigan. There was no talking; we knew the drill. It wasn't that Coach was a monster disciplinarian and that we were scared of him. In fact, it was the opposite. He was a nice guy who treated us fairly. He didn't even have a son of his own on the team. He just coached because he loved the game, so we showed him respect. That meant waiting quietly for his post-game wrap-up.

Madigan came into the room with a load of sticks under his arm. He piled them in the corner, and then he peeled his coat off and threw it on a hook.

"Way to go, fellas! Great game! You just gave the best team in the Greater Toronto Hockey League a real scare. We were a crossbar away from tying the game." He looked around the room, meeting the eyes of each player. We could feel the tension slowly leaving the room. "Last year we were never within five goals of that team. This year, three games into the season, and we're within a hair of a tie."

When Madigan looked at me, he grinned. I was still ticked off about the crossbar and I didn't want to give in and accept the loss. Even so, I found myself beginning to smile too.

"Ya just missed, Jakey," Madigan said. "Don't worry, kid, that one will go in when we need it to."

He turned his attention back to the rest of the team. "Hold your heads high, boys. It's going to be a great year," Madigan said. "Practice Thursday morning at seven. See you then." And just as quickly as he'd entered the room, he headed out the door.

The second he was gone, the boys started in with the chatter and the jokes, and tape balls flew around the room. Most of the guys changed quickly. A lot of them had families that did a bunch of activities and were always rushing off to the next one. My left winger, Lyle Richmond, has two older brothers who play hockey, and a younger sister who's a competitive swimmer. I figure their family must live in their minivan.

I take my time when I get changed. I love the banter and the camaraderie in the locker room. I'm a pretty quiet kid, but I like to listen to the jokes and watch guys whip stuff at each other or drop slushy chunks of ice down the backs of each other's shirts. Next to the ice surface itself, the locker room is one of my favourite places. I feel safe there.

The other slowpoke on the team was our goalie, Freddie Talbot. Long after the rest of the team had cleared out, Freddie and I would still be talking on the bench in the locker room. Freddie's one of my best friends, but he goes to a different school, so the only time we see each other is at hockey.

The door to the room opened and Madigan came back in. "Forgot my coat, jerseys too," he said, collecting the jerseys and putting them into the sweater bag. "I hate to kick you out of here, boys, but your folks are waiting."

Freddie threw his pads over his shoulder and picked up his bag. "Nice game tonight, Jake," he said.

I shouldered my bag and grabbed my sticks. "You too—see you Thursday morning." Then I headed out to the concession area where my parents were waiting.

CHAPTER THREE

On the way home, my dad fiddled with the radio, jumping back and forth between two sports talk-radio stations. One was analyzing the latest woes of the Toronto Maple Leafs, and there seemed to be no end of people calling in to express their opinions. And the whole time Dad talked back to the radio as if he was the one hosting the show.

My dad was a good player when he was younger—great if you listen to his version. Played two years of junior and even had a tryout with the Oshawa Generals, but he never stuck. I forget whether it was his knee or his ankle or his shoulder, lint in his eye or a paper cut, but something stopped him from making the team. This, of course, stopped him from making the NHL. I don't know what he'd do if I stopped playing. Hockey is my dad's life. If he's not watching me play, he's listening to hockey shows on the car radio or watching games on TV. It's a good thing I like the game.

My mom sat silently in the passenger seat and stared straight ahead. She seemed to have forgotten that I was in the van. I spent the ride replaying the game in my mind. I enjoyed thinking about my two goals, especially the "shorty"—it was a beauty. I took a swig of water and watched as a giant eighteen-wheeler in the outside lane slowly moved past us. The memory of my shot ringing off the crossbar made me sigh. I was trying to figure out what I must have done to anger the hockey gods when Dad pulled off the highway. A few minutes later we were parked in our driveway.

I pulled on the sliding van door and called out, "Thanks for the ride, Dad."

He grunted incoherently and slammed his door shut.

I heaved my gear onto my shoulder as Mom came around the front of the van.

"Thanks for watching me play, Mom."

Her face lit up. "Oh, it was my pleasure, Jake. I love to watch you play."

As we walked toward the house together, Mom reached out and put her arm around me.

"Oh, Dude," she groaned and quickly pulled her arm back. "Jake, is that you or your gear?"

"Bit of both," I said, grinning. "Why? Is there a problem?"

"Yeah, there's a problem. You may have scored two goals tonight, but let me be the first to tell you. You stink."

"It's not that bad." I tried to sound offended.

"Trust me, you stink. Hang up your gear and—"

"Rebecca," Dad called. "I'm hungry."

Mom looked like she wanted to say something else, but

instead, she hustled inside to catch up to Dad. I shook my head and went to the basement to hang up my gear.

After dinner, I sat down at my desk. I had a bunch of homework to finish, but before I started, I fired up my computer and went to Google Maps. I punched in the Sault Ste. Marie Greyhounds and took a virtual flight into downtown Sault Ste. Marie. Whenever I was stressed, or in this case, just trying to stall before doing my homework, I would look up a team in the Ontario Hockey League. I'd "fly" in over the town and search out the team's arena. I knew where every rink in the "O" was, but Sault Ste. Marie was my favourite. It seemed mysterious because it's so far up north and so far away from my house. *The farther away, the better,* I thought.

I was only in grade seven and played Major Peewee, but I knew that I was good enough to play in the "O." Every year, the top Midget players from the Greater Toronto Hockey League get drafted into the "O." I've either led the league or been among the top three scorers every year since I started playing. I couldn't wait until my draft year in grade ten. *Three more years,* I told myself as I clicked out of Google.

I threw my history textbook onto my desk and tried to focus on my homework. A lot of the guys on my team struggled with school and were constantly being threatened with the ol' if-you-don't-do-your-homework-you-can't-play line. But those guys had figured out that their parents wouldn't dream of pulling them out of the lineup. It probably meant more to some of the parents that their kid was playing Triple A than it did to the kid himself. My teammates aren't stupid. Some of them were already talking about this being their last year in Triple A. A few of the guys couldn't handle the pressure. Others wanted to snowboard or hang out with girls. Some just knew that only the best of the best would ever go to the next level. In Ontario, that meant playing in the "O."

Come on, Jake, focus, I reminded myself. Why couldn't I have math homework? I like math. I like science; practical subjects. History just confuses me.

I was trying to answer a question about Samuel de Champlain's leadership skills when my bedroom door opened. I glanced over my shoulder to see my dad entering the room. When he turned to close the door, I instinctively stood up to face him.

Dad tried to smile, but I could tell that he was upset. He began to pace back and forth. In my tiny bedroom there wasn't much space, and he kind of reminded me of a caged lion at the zoo.

"Good game tonight, Jake," he said as he ran his hand through his hair.

"Thanks," I answered carefully.

"Yeah, your 'shorty' was a beauty, but that crossbar . . . man, you gotta put that in."

"What?" I wasn't sure I'd heard him correctly.

"You gotta put that in," he repeated.

"You think I missed *on purpose*?" I said.

Dad stopped pacing and spun toward me, grabbing me by the shoulders. "Listen to me," he said. "No scout is gonna be interested in a kid who misses the net with the game on the line."

"Are you kidding me?" I shot back. "You don't think I'll get scouted because I hit the crossbar?"

I brought my left hand up and tried to swat his arms away. As I did, I took a step back to get away from him, but my foot caught on the carpet. At that same moment, Dad shoved me—hard—and I went flying over my desk chair. A lightning bolt of pain seared through my face as I crashed headfirst into the wooden shelving unit hanging above my desk. The corner of a shelf sliced open my cheek. Several trophies crashed to the desk below.

"Aaahh!" I cried out, grabbing my face as I crumpled to the floor.

Dad stood over me. "Jake, you okay, buddy?" He was using that fake, cheerful voice he uses when he knows that he's done something wrong. "Come on, buddy. Let me have a look."

"Leave me alone," I growled.

Dad blew out his breath in frustration. "Fine, lie there. But someday you're gonna have to learn to toughen up." I heard his footsteps as he turned and walked out into the hallway.

I lay on the floor for a long time, waiting for my breathing to slow down. I winced at the pain that was throbbing in my face and shook my head, trying to shake it off. There was no way I would give my dad the satisfaction of hearing me cry. Finally, I pushed myself to my feet and took a few shaky steps. Out in the hallway, I could see the light from the TV flickering in my parents' room.

That's nice, I thought. *Shove me into a shelf, cut my face, and then go watch* SportsLine.

I slipped into the bathroom that separates my parents' room

from mine and groaned when I looked in the mirror. A nasty-looking red scrape ran from the edge of my right eye back to my ear. I cursed under my breath and was just about to splash water on my face, when I paused. I could hear voices coming through the air vent above the shower. Years ago, I'd learned that I could hear Mom and Dad from there when they were talking in their room, but eavesdropping on them had never interested me much. Now however, I moved toward the vent and stood perfectly still. Very quietly but very clearly, there came the sound of my parents' voices.

"Jeff," Mom was saying, "I just want to see if he's okay."

My dad snorted. "He doesn't want any help. Don't you see what I'm doing here, Rebecca?"

If Mom answered, I couldn't hear her.

"I'm building character," my dad went on. "I was just talking to him about the game; you know, trying to help him be a better player, and he got all snippy with me. Trust me, one day he'll thank me for trying to toughen him up."

I listened for a few more minutes, but all I could hear was the television. Apparently Dad's lecture was over. I let out an irritated sigh and turned on the tap. As I splashed water on my face, I tried to imagine a time when I would ever thank my dad for "toughening me up." I was pretty sure that the day would never come.

Back in my bedroom, I was way too wound up to sleep. I paced back and forth as I tried to clear my head. For as long as I could remember my dad had been in my face. He pushed me about everything. If I got B's in school, he wanted A's. He demanded to know where I was, who I spent my time with, what we were doing, and why we were doing it. I figured that I was the most closely watched kid in North York. But it was with my hockey that he took crazy to a whole new level. When I was younger, I had to shoot two hundred pucks a night in the basement, and if I didn't score in a game I wasn't allowed to watch TV until I scored again. I learned to score in games just before a long break in the schedule.

The first time Dad hit me was after my team lost a game in Novice. I had been more confused than hurt that time. It was just a slap across the small of my back, but I can still remember being eight years old and trying to figure out why Dad had been so angry about me losing at hockey. Looking back, I honestly think he tried to control his temper, but he just got so wrapped up in the sport. And the more important the game, the more likely he was to snap if we didn't win. It had gotten to the point where I just never knew how he was going to react afterwards. What was he going to do when I told him that instead of trying for a scholarship to an American university like he wanted, I wanted to play in the "O"?

That's when I noticed it. My old, worn-out backpack spilling out from my closet. I carried it over to my bed and sat down.

How much can this thing hold? I wondered.

I pulled a thick sweater out of my dresser and stuffed it into the bottom of the backpack. Then I piled in several pairs of socks and a pair of long underwear. The more I stuffed into the backpack, the more my mind began to race. At the very best, all I could hope to get my hands on would be a few water bottles and maybe some granola bars.

Then what?

I sat down at my desk and pulled open the top drawer. That was where I kept my stash of money from Christmases and birthdays. I sorted through the bills, and my heart sank. I had a whopping eighty-five dollars to my name. If I wanted to buy a new hockey stick, then eighty-five bucks would be all right, but as an escape fund? I'd need a lot more money than that.

Feeling defeated, I peeled off my clothes and pulled on my pyjamas. I flopped onto my bed, mad at myself for even considering that running away could ever be a possibility.

Where would you go, Jake? I asked myself.

I had nowhere to go, barely any money, and no food. Eventually I fell asleep, listing all the reasons why running away would be a really stupid idea.

CHAPTER FOUR

The next morning I woke from a troubled sleep. When I was little I used to have this dream. It was always the same. I'd be standing on this rickety little walkway thing, which was suspended way up in the air, and I never knew why but I had to cross it. The funny thing is that I'm terrified of heights so it seemed weird that I'd be there. The dream always ended the same way: I felt compelled to cross the walkway, yet partway across I would fall. When I was really little, I'd wake up screaming. It freaked out my mom, but our family doctor told her that I'd outgrow it. Last night I didn't scream, but I did dream, I did fall, and I woke up terrified.

Groggily, I sat up and tried to collect my thoughts. The room was blurry. When I wiped the sleep from my eyes, a pain shot through the right side of my face, and I remembered. I staggered to the bathroom and looked in the mirror. While I had slept, the eye had swollen completely shut and was now a sickening combination of black, red, and dark purple.

"Oh this is just perfect," I muttered to the nasty-looking reflection in the mirror.

After ten minutes in the shower, my eye slowly began to open and my head started to clear. I would have a lot of explaining to do when I got to school. As I let the water flow over me, I ran through all the excuses that I could think of. Not one of them seemed remotely believable.

I dressed quickly and headed down to the kitchen. Mom was busy making my lunch. "Good morning, honey . . ." she started, but her sentence trailed off when she saw my eye. "Oh, no." She moved toward me and stretched out her arms, like she wanted to hug me.

Instinctively my hands came up. "Don't touch me," I muttered.

Mom stopped dead in her tracks, and through my one good eye I could see the look of pain that crossed her face. I'd hurt her feelings, but I was too angry to care.

"You never even came to see if I was okay."

"I . . . I wanted to," she said.

"But you didn't."

Mom's shoulders sagged. "You're right. I'm sorry." She raised her arms again. "Can I check you now?"

I wasn't sure that I wanted to be hugged, but I let my mom come closer. She squeezed me tight and gave me a gentle kiss on the forehead. Her eyes were misty, but she forced a smile and whispered, "Everything's going to be okay."

"Rebecca, is my lunch ready?" Dad demanded as he came into the kitchen.

Mom and I both started at the sound of his voice. Mom

quickly broke off our hug and hustled over to the counter to grab Dad's lunch. "Here you go," she said.

"Thanks," he replied. "I gotta go." He looked at me as if he'd just realized that I was in the room. "Whoa, buddy, that's quite the shiner. Look, I'm sorry that you hurt yourself, but can you do me a favour and tell your teacher that . . ." His voice trailed off.

I glared at him. "Tell him what?" I asked.

Dad studied my face for a moment. "I dunno, maybe you took a hockey stick in the eye or something?"

I shrugged. "I guess that's what happened."

He nodded, and for a moment he actually looked a little sad. "Yeah, I guess that's what happened," he repeated quietly. "I gotta go," he told Mom. "I'll see you tonight." Then he turned and left.

An hour later I walked purposefully onto the school playground. I looked around, thankful that it was a sunny day; it gave me an excuse to wear sunglasses. I tugged hard on my San Jose Sharks baseball cap and pulled it down low on my forehead. Then I headed toward a group of my friends who were standing around waiting for the bell to ring.

A tall, skinny boy smiled as I approached. "Jakey," he said.

I nodded back. "How's it going, Stilts?"

Stilts, whose real name was Caleb, shrugged his shoulders. "Good, you?"

No one else in the group noticed me. They were too self-absorbed in their own conversations or trying to deafen themselves with their iPods. I was thankful for their indifference because I was still trying to check for any flaws in the hockey-stick-to-the-eye story. I had learned, over the years, that if I didn't want people snooping around in my private life, my excuses needed to be flawless. I wasn't sure why, but something about this story bothered me. When the bell sounded, we lined up and waited for a teacher to come and open the doors. Eventually Mr. Hamilton arrived with a cheerful "Good morning, everybody."

Some of the students greeted Mr. Hamilton with a smile and a "good morning," but most of them just dragged their feet sleepily down the hall toward their classrooms.

Outside the classroom I slung my backpack up onto a hook and pulled out my pencil case and books. Then I hesitated. I thought about leaving the cap and glasses on. But Hamilton was sure to ask me to take them off and that would draw even more attention to the shiner.

I put them up on the shelf above the hook and waited to see what would happen. I didn't have to wait long.

"Holy smokes, Jake. What happened?" Stilts asked.

"Took a hockey stick in the eye last night."

"Brutal! Does it hurt?"

"No, I'm good," I answered, trying to sound cheerful. I quickly headed for the classroom.

In my rush to get to my seat, I accidentally bumped into one of my classmates, a small blonde girl named Samantha, knocking her books and school supplies to the floor. Sam and I had been in school together since kindergarten, and sitting beside each other since the third grade. Outside of my hockey teammates, Sam was my best friend. She was that one person I always felt comfortable talking to.

"Sorry, Sam," I mumbled.

I scooped up her case and handed it to her.

"Thanks," she began, then noticed my eye. "Oh my God," she whispered.

"It's okay," I responded defensively.

"What happened?"

"I took a stick in the eye last night."

"Are you all right?"

I gave her my best smile, which really didn't work in light of my hideously bruised face.

"I'm good, Sam."

Sam continued to study me. I had an uneasy feeling that she wasn't buying my story. "Jake—"

"Sam, I'm fine. It was just a high stick." I turned and headed into the class.

Sam took her seat beside me. I was already copying out the day's word problem. This was designed to keep us busy while Mr. Hamilton took attendance, hot dog orders, and pizza orders, and collected money for a number of different activities.

Today's question was: *You throw away the outside and cook the inside. Then you eat the outside and throw away the inside. What is it?*

I leaned over my desk and rested my head in my free hand while I copied the question. I could feel Sam watching me, but I kept my head down and tried not to look at her.

"Okay, class, let's get started," Mr. Hamilton said. "Does anyone have an answer to the word problem?"

Hands shot up around the room and Mr. Hamilton called on each one in turn. The first kid suggested an egg, but this answer was dismissed because it only fit the first part of the statement: *you throw away the outside* would be the shell, *and cook the inside*. It didn't satisfy the second part of the question because once the egg was eaten there would be nothing left to throw away.

Stilts raised his hand.

"A fish," he answered confidently.

"Interesting, Caleb," Hamilton answered. "Can you explain your answer?"

"Sure. *You throw away the outside* would be the scales or the skin, and *you throw away the inside* would be the bones."

"But you'd cook the skin with the fish, so it wouldn't get thrown away," someone called from the back of the room.

"Well, I like my answer!" Stilts said defiantly.

"Take it easy," Hamilton laughed. He looked around the room. "Come on, people, you're so close."

I loved this part of the day, the challenge of trying to solve the daily problem. I was pretty sure that I had the right answer and was dying to raise my hand, but kept my head down. Hamilton's eyes finally landed on Sam and me.

"Sam?" he asked hopefully.

Sam smiled and shrugged. "I got nothing, Mr. Hamilton."

"Fair enough." I could feel Mr. Hamilton looking at me. "Any ideas, Jake?"

I kept my head lowered as I said, "A cob of corn, sir."

"Well done," he said, sounding relieved that someone had solved his problem. "So tell us, what is the outside?"

"The husk," I mumbled.

"Correct. Then you cook the inside. And then what?"

I shifted uncomfortably under my teacher's gaze. "Well, you

eat the corn, and then you throw away the cob." I still hadn't made eye contact with my teacher.

"Jake?" he asked.

"Yes, sir?"

"Are you feeling okay?"

Once again, I muttered my answer into my desktop. "Yes, I'm fine."

Hamilton tried again. "Jake? Do you think you could do me the courtesy of looking at me when I'm talking to you?"

Here we go, I thought. Slowly I raised my head, thankful that Sam and I sat at the front of the room. When Hamilton saw my eye he let out a startled, "Whoa!"

The kids that sat behind us struggled to see what all the fuss was about. I wanted to slide off my chair and crawl under my desk.

"Are you all right?" he asked.

"Yeah, I'm fine. It's no big deal."

"Goodness, what happened?" Hamilton asked.

"I took a hockey stick in the eye last night."

He nodded sympathetically. I knew that he thought hockey was barbaric, but I could tell that he believed my story. He also looked really worried about me.

"Does it hurt?" he asked.

Yeah, it hurts, my head is throbbing. "No, it's okay," I answered quietly.

"Have you had any ice on it yet?"

I shook my head.

Hamilton threw up his hands, "Well, no wonder it looks like a month-old banana."

Some of the kids laughed, but stopped when they realized that Hamilton wasn't trying to be funny.

"Sam," he said, "would you go down to the office and get Jake some ice for his eye, please?"

As she stood up, Sam took one more look at me. I already had my head buried in my hand again and was doodling in my workbook. If anyone could tell I was lying, it would be Sam. I refused to look up at her. Finally, she headed for the classroom door.

CHAPTER FIVE

At five thirty the next morning my alarm clock signalled the start of a new day. Today was a hockey day and I couldn't wait. I saw no difference between games and practices. I just loved to be on the ice. It was the one place where I always felt safe. Even cutting hard to the net with my head down against hostile defencemen didn't scare me. Hockey was where my friends were. It was where my coaches were. It was where I was the best player in a rink full of guys who would die to be as good as me. It was where I had fun.

I dressed quickly and headed for the kitchen. I was surprised to see my mom leaning against the counter, sipping her coffee. In all my years of playing, she had hardly ever gotten up for a morning practice. That had always been Dad's responsibility.

"Good morning, honey. How'd you sleep?"

I grabbed a bowl from the cupboard for cereal. "Pretty good," I lied. My head hadn't stopped throbbing since I'd woken up yesterday.

I was just digging into my breakfast when my father came into the kitchen.

"Morning, Rebecca," he said. "I'm surprised to see you up."

"Well," she answered, "I was thinking I would take Jake to his practice."

Dad reached into the cupboard and pulled out a bowl. His back was still to Mom when he said, "Oh yeah? Now why would you want to do that?"

"Oh, I don't know. I guess I just felt like watching Jake skate."

Her answer sounded rehearsed, even to me, and I stopped chewing and held my breath.

Dad poured himself some cereal, opened a drawer, and pulled out a spoon. "Really? After seven years of hockey you suddenly want to go to a morning practice?" He turned around to look at her with a strange smile on his face.

Mom hesitated, then said, "Maybe . . . maybe it's time that I helped out a bit with the driving."

Dad's smile disappeared as he continued to stare at Mom. "I've got the driving," he said firmly. Then he pushed past her and sat down at the kitchen table. Without even looking at me, he said, "The van leaves in ten minutes. Make sure your gear is loaded up and you're ready to go."

I got up from the table and rushed to grab my stuff.

On the way to the rink Dad ignored me as he repeatedly jabbed his finger into the preset buttons for the sports radio shows. I looked out the window. Years ago, I had learned to view my dad the way you should view a sleeping bear: if the bear is quiet, best not to disturb it. So I kept my mouth shut and my thoughts to myself.

As we pulled into the parking lot, Dad said, "How was school yesterday?"

Uh-oh, I thought. *Where's he going with this?*

"It was fine," I answered carefully.

"What did your teacher think about your eye?"

Now I knew what he was after. He wanted to know if anyone was questioning my story.

"He was worried about me, got me some ice."

"That was nice of him," Dad said. He seemed edgy. He parked the van and turned to face me. "Sometimes I'm pretty hard on you, but you know why I do it, right?"

Because you're crazy?

"I'm doing it for your own good," Dad said. "I'm trying to toughen you up; develop your character. Someday you'll understand."

I was pretty sure I understood that he was psycho, but again, I just looked out the window. "Dad, I'm gonna be late," I answered.

"Right, right. You don't want to keep your coach waiting. Get going. Go and have some fun. And remember to put the puck in the net."

I grabbed my gear and headed for the rink. *Remember to put the puck in the net? How could I ever forget?*

The first thing Freddie Talbot noticed when he walked into the dressing room was my eye. "Holy, Jake, what happened to you?"

"Took a stick in the eye," I responded absently.

Freddie dropped his gear beside mine and flopped down on the bench. "You okay?"

"Yeah, I'm good."

Every player that came in noticed my eye and asked what had happened. Before long, Freddie had turned it into a game where he tried to offer a different explanation to each. By the time the last guy had entered the room, I had slipped in the shower, walked into a door, been in a knife fight, fallen out of a tree, been hit by a baseball, and rescued an old lady from a burning building.

Freddie was doing a great job of entertaining everyone, but he was really stressing me out. My head was pounding and the last thing I needed was Freddie drawing attention to my eye by making stupid jokes. I really wished that he would just shut his mouth. The laughter finally ended when Coach Madigan came into the room to talk to us before practice. He was explaining a breakout drill that we were going to work on when he noticed me and stopped mid-sentence. After a moment he regained his composure.

"I'm good, Coach," I said, before he could ask.

"What happened?"

Freddie answered, "A ninja attacked him on his way home from school."

The rest of the boys laughed, but Madigan didn't see the humour. He glared at Freddie and the team fell silent.

"Seriously, Jake, what happened?"

"I took a hockey stick in the eye, Coach."

Madigan raised his eyebrows. "I didn't notice that the other night. And anyway, how could that happen when you wear a full cage when you play?"

Oh no, I thought as my stomach flipped. I suddenly realized what it was about my story that had been bothering me. I scrambled quickly for a reasonable answer. I could feel every guy in the room staring at me and I had to resist the urge to panic. *Think, Jake. And make it quick.* An idea came to me.

"I was playing road hockey, Coach."

Madigan continued to stare at me and somehow I knew that he didn't believe me. After what felt like forever, he said, "Okay, boys, let's get started."

I didn't want to give Madigan any more time to think about my eye. I knew that as soon as we got out on the ice, the only thing on his mind would be breakouts and defensive zone coverage. I jumped up and hustled for the door.

Our fourth game of the season was against the Etobicoke Flames. Ever since Novice, the Toronto Eagles and Etobicoke had battled it out each year to see who would finish first and earn a trip to the All Ontario Championships. The other teams in the league fought for the right to finish third, a long way behind the top two teams.

As usual, I arrived early at the rink. I leaned my shoulder into the dressing room door and dragged my equipment bag and sticks behind me. The room was empty except for Freddie and Coach Madigan.

Freddie looked up at me and smiled. "Hey, Jakey."

I tossed my equipment down beside his and took a seat.

"How's it going, Freddie?"

Madigan was walking around the room, hanging up our jerseys. He came over and handed mine to me.

"Thanks, Coach," I said.

"Jakey, are your folks here?" Madigan asked.

I nodded.

"Let's go talk to them, okay?" he said.

Uh-oh, I thought. *This can't be good.*

I followed him out into the warm viewing area.

Mom was standing near the concession stand. She was sipping coffee and talking to Freddie's mom.

"Afternoon," Madigan said. "Rebecca, do you have a second?"

I saw her blink in confusion as she darted a glance at me. Then her eyes went back to Madigan and she said brightly, "Absolutely, Coach."

Mom and I followed Madigan over to the viewing windows, where Dad was sitting by himself watching a Midget team practice.

"Jeff, can we talk?" Madigan asked.

"What's on your mind, Coach?"

"I'm worried about Jake's eye—"

"He's fine," Dad interrupted.

"Okay," Madigan answered, calmly. "Just wanted to be sure. I probably shouldn't have let him practise the other day, but it was first thing in the morning; kind of caught me off guard. Did you take him to the hospital? Get him checked out?"

Dad laughed nervously and turned back to watch the practice. "It was just a high stick in a road hockey game."

Madigan turned to me, and he was no longer smiling.

"How are you feeling, Jake?" he asked.

My head had been aching for three days, but I answered cheerfully. "I'm ready to play, Coach."

"Jake," he said, "your eye is still swollen nearly shut. You could have damage to your orbital bone. You could even be concussed. I'm not sure you should play."

Before I could answer, Dad stood up and faced Madigan. He ran his hand through his hair and took a deep breath. "Listen, Coach, he's fine," he said.

I could tell that he was working to keep his voice down.

Madigan hesitated. "Well, maybe I should have our trainer look at him before he plays—"

Dad cut him off. "I'll tell you what. If Jake looks shaky in the first period, then you can pull him out. But let him play. You'll see. He's fine."

Madigan didn't look convinced, but he agreed. "Thanks for your time, Jeff." He smiled at Mom. "Rebecca."

I was about to follow Madigan back to the dressing room when Dad dropped his hand onto my shoulder.

"Have a great game, son," he said, a little too loudly and a little too cheerfully. Then he leaned down and quietly spoke in my ear, "And don't forget to put the puck in the net."

"You know what? I'd probably have a better chance if I could see out of both eyes," I said. Before he could say anything else, I headed for the dressing room.

When we took the ice for warm-up, I could feel tension in the air. As we skated around in our end of the rink, I cast an eye over at the Flames players. They looked different than usual.

Lyle skated past me and said, "Is it just me, or do they look nervous?"

"The Flames nervous of us? Not likely."

"Well," he said, "maybe they heard about our game with Toronto."

"I'm sure they did, but I can't imagine they're scared of us." I was still worrying about Madigan pulling me out of the game. I was worried about how much my head was aching. I didn't have time to worry about whether or not the Flames were nervous.

After the game started, I began to think that maybe Lyle was right, because Etobicoke seemed tight right from the drop of the puck. I scored early on a pretty soft shot and added a second goal just before the end of the first period. Early in the second, Etobicoke mustered their first decent chance, but Freddie made an incredible save. That was the last one they had. I scored two more goals in the second period, and when Madigan told me that he was going to rest me for the third period, I didn't argue. My headache eased a bit as I watched my teammates cruise to an easy 6–0 victory.

When Coach Madigan walked into the dressing room after the game, we were doing our best to wait quietly for him. A huge smile creased his face, and he gave a big fist pump.

"Way to go, boys!" he yelled.

The team erupted into a huge cheer. Madigan beamed and looked around the room at each of us.

"What do you say for Freddie, boys? First shutout of the year!"

Again the room filled with cheers.

"Hey, Coach!" Freddie shouted above the roar of his teammates. "That's the first time we've ever beat Etobicoke." Freddie was our stats man. If you needed hockey history, you asked him.

"No kiddin'," Madigan replied. He still wore a smile.

"Nope, we tied them once in Novice, but that was as close as we ever came."

A series of shouts and whoops went up again and Madigan had to yell to get us to be quiet. When the room settled down, he continued.

"Listen, boys, I'm really proud of you, but remember that this was just one game. We're already three and one, and I think that we're going to have an incredible season." He paused for a moment as he reached into his briefcase. He rummaged inside, then pulled out some papers that he passed around.

"Because we're going to be so good this year, I have a job I need you to do. This is a fundraiser form for a meat order. I need you guys to get out there and sell some meat."

"What for, Coach?" Lyle asked.

"All the money raised will go directly to the team," Madigan answered. "And this isn't all we're gonna do. We're gonna have car washes, we'll sell chocolate bars. We'll do everything we can to raise money because there's a tournament that I want to take you guys to."

I gave the room a scan. Everybody was listening intently.

"What tournament?" Joseph Winslow asked.

Madigan smiled. "It's a surprise."

We let out a collective groan.

"Aw, come on, Coach," Freddie protested.

Madigan held up his hands. "Listen, it's a surprise. That's all I'm gonna tell you. And don't bother asking your parents. They've been sworn to secrecy, and if they tell you, they know that I'll bench you as punishment."

We laughed as Madigan continued. "There are two things that I need you to do this year. I need you to keep winning, and I need you to raise some money. Now have a great night. That was a huge win."

Before any of us could ask any more questions, he walked out of the room. The second that he was gone, we started in with the chatter. But tonight there was no horseplay. We were all too busy trying to guess where Coach's mystery tournament could be.

"Wherever it is," Freddie said, "it must be big."

I had to agree. I felt like nothing was going to stop me. Not my dad, not a black eye—nothing. I'd sell meat, I'd raise money, and I'd continue to score goals. I could handle anything that was thrown at me. This was going to be a great year.

CHAPTER SIX

Our team picked up steam and continued to roll over our opponents. By the tenth game of the year we had improved our record to nine and one. By then I was leading the league in scoring with fifteen goals and eighteen assists for thirty-three points. Each time I took the ice I burned with a desire to control the play. I blocked shots, I threw punishing bodychecks, I made amazing tape-to-tape passes through legs and over sticks that somehow always seemed to find an open teammate. And I scored: dekes, dangles, roof jobs, and slappers were all part of my repertoire. The more I thought about Madigan's secret tournament the harder I played, and the harder I played, the more we won.

One day in the middle of October, North York and most of Southern Ontario were greeted by a beautiful summer-like day. Most of the students at my school arrived in shorts and T-shirts, happy for one last gasp of summer before the long, dreary days of winter set in. As the class began to work on Mr. Hamilton's word problem, no one seemed to notice that I wasn't wearing bright shorts and a colourful T-shirt. In fact, I was the only one in class who was wearing jeans and long sleeves.

Sam plunked herself down beside me and reached into her desk for her math supplies. "Morning, Jake," she said. "Isn't it a great day?" She had on bright pink shorts with giant white flowers and a bright red shirt that had an angry looking pirate on the front beside the slogan *I survived summer vacation with my parents and our AAAARRRRRRRRR-VEE.*

She looks kinda like a giant Valentine's card, I thought. Then our eyes met, and for some reason I couldn't remember what it was I had just been thinking about.

"Jake?"

"Uh . . . yeah. Morning, Sam. You look really colourful . . . I mean nice."

Sam laughed. "Thanks for noticing, Jake. But why aren't you wearing shorts today?"

"I didn't realize how warm it was," I answered. Before Sam could say anything else I gave a quick tug on my sleeves and turned my attention back to the word problem.

Our class ended with a gym period. I love phys. ed. Anything that involves running, throwing, or catching is good by me. Since it was such a beautiful day, Mr. Hamilton said he'd take the class outside for a game of flag football. My classmates scurried about, stacking their chairs and cleaning up their desks.

I really want to play, I thought. *But I can't.* I went over to Hamilton's desk.

He threw the lanyard with his whistle on over his head and looked up at me. "Something on your mind, Jake?"

"I forgot my gym clothes," I answered.

Hamilton was usually pretty strict about gym clothes. He said it was bad enough that he spent his days with a bunch of crazy adolescents, but if we smelled like sweat and body odour too, then that was just downright cruel. But he smiled at me and said, "That's okay, Jake. We're going outside anyway. Why don't you participate in the clothes you've got on?"

"Umm . . ."

"Something wrong?"

I shook my head.

"Not feeling well?"

"No. Is it okay if I sit out?"

"No problem, Jake," Hamilton said, heading for the door. He called to the rest of the class as he passed through the door. "Hurry up, everybody, it's a beautiful day. Let's get outside and enjoy it."

I sighed, grabbed my backpack, and shuffled along after my classmates.

Sitting by myself in the sun, I watched as everyone else battled it out in a spirited game of flag football. I could see that Sam was playing half-heartedly. She was the smallest kid in class, and she made no secret about the fact that she didn't like sports.

"Mr. Hamilton!" she yelled. "May I get a drink of water, please?"

Hamilton was busy quarterbacking for both teams because he said the boys never passed to the girls. "Go ahead, Sam," he called.

Sam grabbed her water bottle and wandered over to where I was sitting. She sat down beside me. "How's it going?"

"I hate sitting out," I muttered.

"Then, don't forget your gym clothes," she teased.

A small smile was trying to form at the corner of my mouth.

"And look on the bright side," she added. "The weather's great, and you're not in history class."

I took a deep breath and put my hands behind me. Leaning back, I stretched out my legs, tilted my face to the sun, and closed my eyes. "Okay, Sam, you're the boss."

"Don't you forget it."

I heard Sam get up, but after a minute or two, I could still feel her standing over me. With my eyes closed, I said, "Shouldn't you get back to the game?"

"You've seen me try to catch," she answered. "Mr. Hamilton will never notice that I'm gone."

"All right, stay here and keep me company. We'll watch to see if Stilts can run in a straight line without tripping."

"Right," Sam said. "So, Jake . . ." She suddenly sounded nervous as she sat back down beside me. "What have you been up to lately?"

"Same old, same old," I answered. "Hockey, hockey, hockey."

"You guys any good this year?" she asked.

"Thirteen and one."

"Did you play last night?"

"Yep."

"If you're thirteen and one, I suppose you won."

"Yeah, we beat Leaside 2–1 yesterday. They outplayed us, but our goalie was terrific."

"How'd *you* play?"

Again, she sounded nervous to me. *What's with her?* I thought. *Oh no!*

My eyes flew open and I could see Sam studying my arms. I sat up and pulled my sleeves back down. "I played okay, I guess." It was actually the first game all year that I didn't have a point.

"Was it a rough game?" she asked.

"Not really. Why?"

"I just noticed that you've got some bad bruises on your arms."

"Oh, that." I laughed nervously. "Yeah, I got slashed."

Sam stood up again. "Must have been quite a slash to hit you on both wrists at the same time," she said as she walked off.

We won our next game over the lowly Mississauga Warriors, but I was struggling. I'd turned into a bundle of nerves on the ice. I was normally so sure-handed, but against Mississauga I looked like I was trying to stickhandle a hand grenade. Late in the game I was wide open at the side of the net and missed an easy tap in.

The problem started after that Leaside game, when I didn't score. Dad ended up getting so freaked out that he grabbed me by the wrists. The more I tried to pull away the tighter he held on. And then Sam saw the bruises. Now I was more worried than ever about how my dad would react if I didn't play well, and I was also worried that Sam might tell someone about my wrists. No wonder I missed the stupid net against Mississauga.

After the game, Madigan congratulated us on the win and began to pass out his newest fundraiser.

"What is it this time, Coach?" Freddie asked.

"Batteries," Madigan announced.

"Batteries?" Freddie laughed.

"Yup, everybody needs batteries. Now get out there and sell, sell, sell."

"Where are we going again, Coach?" Freddie asked.

"Nice try, Freddie," Madigan said. "Hustle up, guys, it's a school night. Oh, and Jake, can I see you before you go?"

"Sure, Coach."

After the room emptied, Madigan sat down on the bench with me.

"You okay, Jake?" he asked. "You just didn't seem like yourself out there tonight."

"Bad game, I guess."

Madigan smiled. "Well, we all have a bad game once in a while."

I nodded. I wasn't sure where he was going with this, but I had learned over the years that when people were asking me questions, the less said the better.

"Don't worry about it, Jake," he said, standing up. "You always score when we need it."

I got up and hefted my hockey bag.

"Oh, and Jake?" Madigan added. "If there's anything you ever want to talk about, I'd be happy to listen."

I gave him my best I-have-no-idea-what-you're-talking-about look and picked up my sticks. I was at the dressing room door when I said, "Coach?"

"Yeah, Jake?"

"Thanks."

"For what?" Madigan asked.

Without looking back at him, I said, "For caring." Before he could say anything else, I yanked on the door and rushed out of the rink.

Later that night, I was in my bedroom finishing off my homework when my door opened. I fought to control the fear that swept through me as I stood up to face my dad. But he just walked over to my trophy display. He picked up an MVP trophy from some tournament and studied it.

"Another big win," he said.

I stayed motionless at my desk, not sure if I was supposed to answer him.

Dad continued to study my trophies. "Fourteen and one," he said, more to the display case than to me. "Do you know what your record was after fifteen games last year, Jake?"

I was pretty sure that whatever I said would be wrong, but I also knew that he expected an answer. "No," I replied.

"Eight and seven," he answered.

"Good improvement."

"How many points do you have, Jake?"

"Thirty-six," I answered.

"Thirty-six," he repeated. "How many points did you have after ten games?"

Here it comes. I knew that I should know the answer. I always knew how many points I had, but suddenly I couldn't remember anything. "I don't know," I said.

"You *don't know*?" Dad challenged. "Let me remind you. You had thirty-three points."

He was still holding the trophy and now he took a step

toward me. "How many points do you have in your last five games? It's pretty easy math," he added sarcastically.

"Three," I said.

Dad scoffed. "Three points, but none in your last two games. That's not very good, is it." He took a quick step toward me and raised the trophy.

I squeezed my eyes shut and ducked to avoid the hit. When nothing happened, I opened my eyes and there was Dad holding the trophy just inches in front of my face. It shook in his hand.

"Guys who don't score points don't win trophies. Guys who don't score points don't get drafted." He placed the trophy back on the shelf, and just like that, left the room.

I stared at the door, so mad and scared and confused that I wanted to scream. Rage burned in my stomach, and I think that was the only thing that kept me from crying.

I can't take much more of this, I thought. I reached down and pulled open my desk drawer. Ever since Dad injured my eye on the bookshelf, I had been sneaking water bottles and granola bars out of the kitchen. The more I thought about running away, the more I realized that it was a ridiculous idea, but somehow it always made me feel better to put more supplies into my backpack. I moved my latest stash from the desk into the pack, then hid it in the closet again. By the time I closed the closet door, my hands had stopped shaking.

I crawled into bed, fluffed up my pillow, and turned out the light.

That night, I dreamed that I had run away. I seemed to be running up a hill, climbing higher and higher. Suddenly, I found myself at the old rickety walkway from my recurring dream.

Maybe I can run across it, I thought. Gathering my courage I started to sprint, but about halfway across, I tripped and fell. Just as I was about to smash onto the ground, I woke up, terrified and exhausted.

CHAPTER SEVEN

As October gave way to November, the Peewee division of the GTHL was once again a two-horse race. However, this year there was a new horse competing. After our early-season heartbreaker against the Toronto Eagles—I still had nightmares about my shot ricocheting off the crossbar—my North York Penguins were matching the Eagles, win for win. Despite my mini slump, I was still leading the league in scoring. Freddie was giving us incredible goaltending, and we were playing solid team defence. The only blemish on Toronto's record was a 4–4 tie with the Etobicoke Flames. After twenty games the Eagles had put together an incredible record of nineteen wins, no losses, and one tie for thirty-nine out of a possible forty points.

After nineteen games, we had thirty-six points. Our twentieth game of the season was a rematch with Etobicoke. The Flames sat third in the league with thirty-three points. I knew they were going to be hungry. A win would put them right behind us in the standings. A loss, and they would fall that much further behind.

I had a surge of adrenaline as I skated around for warm-up. I'd had that feeling lots of times before, and whenever it happened, I always felt quicker, my legs lighter. Maybe the slump that had been dogging me lately was about to snap.

Unfortunately, once the game started, it turned into a battle between the blue lines. Neither team was able to generate much in the way of offence. The goalies were left with only a few decent scoring chances to deal with as both teams forechecked hard and backchecked harder.

By the time the third period started, the Flames were clearly getting tired. It takes a lot of energy to play at such a physical level throughout an entire game. With each shift, I had a bit more open ice and a bit more room to move. Late in the game, I grabbed the puck and took off, heading for the neutral zone. A defenceman tried to cut me off, but I swerved hard to the right and kept skating up the right wall. As I crossed over their blue line, I wound up and unleashed a slapshot. The goalie hadn't even moved when the puck bulged the twine in the back of the net. I let out a whoop and threw my arms up to celebrate. My second goal went in at the last minute when the Flames pulled their goalie in a desperate attempt to tie the game. For the second time that year, Freddie shut out Etobicoke. More importantly, we stayed within one point of the Toronto Eagles.

As the season wore on, the Eagles continued to dominate the rest of the GTHL and we managed to stick with them. That made our rematch on December 14 that much more crucial. At our final practice before the big game, Coach Madigan put us through a very high-energy session, focusing on defensive zone coverage. "We have to limit their chances," he kept saying.

Back in the dressing room, Madigan came in and called for quiet. "Listen up. I have an announcement."

"You gonna finally tell us about this mystery tournament, Coach?" Freddie asked jokingly.

"Actually I am, Freddie."

I had been slouched on the bench trying to catch my breath after the workout, but now I sat bolt upright, listening intently.

Madigan noticed and laughed. "I thought that might get your attention. Boys, we've worked really hard this year, on and off the ice. You've played great hockey, and we've fundraised like there was no tomorrow. Now our whole season comes down to one game."

Like me, all the guys were hanging onto Coach's every word.

"I wasn't sure if I should tell you before the Eagles game or wait until afterwards, but I felt that it was important for you to realize the significance of this game. The tournament that I want to take you to is by invitation only. The team from the GTHL that has the best record as of December the fifteenth gets a spot in the Triple A Elite division of the Quebec Peewee Tournament."

Instantly, the boys were buzzing with excitement. I was stunned. The Quebec Peewee Tournament! For minor hockey players it was the biggest tournament in the world.

Madigan called for quiet again. "Guys, we're gonna go to this tournament no matter what. That's why we've been fundraising so much. We can go to Quebec and play in a lower level and we'll have a great time, or we can play in the top division against the best teams in the world. We're talking about teams from the USA, Russia, Sweden, and Finland. All we have to do is beat the Toronto Eagles this weekend."

His face turned serious. "What do you think, can we do it?" he challenged.

The team responded with a deafening "Yeah!"

I yelled the loudest of all. One win for a trip to the Quebec Peewee Tournament? I smiled to myself. *We can do one win.*

After Madigan stunned us with his news about the Quebec Peewee Tournament, Freddie and I changed, then plunked ourselves down on the bench with our legs stretched out on top of our hockey bags.

"Pretty exciting stuff, huh?" I said.

"Quebec will be awesome," Freddie said. "Are you guys studying it in history?"

I laughed. Leave it to Freddie to think about the historical significance of the City of Quebec. "Yeah, we are, but who cares? We're not going there for school."

Freddie looked shocked. "Who cares? Jake, the city is over four hundred years old. Think of the history, think of the culture!"

"Think of the scouts," I said. "Think of the opportunity to play the best players in the world."

Freddie stared down at his feet.

"What's wrong?" I asked.

"Jake, I think you need to accept the fact that we won't be playing in the elite division."

"What are you talking about?" I asked.

"Oh, come on!" Freddie exclaimed. "We've never beaten the Eagles."

"Well, I guess we're due!" I smiled.

Freddie just snarled at me. "That's right, go ahead and joke."

He was usually an extremely relaxed guy and his anger took me by surprise. "What's your problem?" I asked.

Slowly, Freddie said. "I'm . . . I'm the goalie."

I laughed. "Yeah, you're the goalie. So?"

"If you have a bad game someone else can pick up the slack. But with a goalie, no one picks up the slack. Either I stop the puck or we lose."

"You'll stop the puck," I said. "And don't worry—you won't have to be perfect because I'm gonna light it up."

Freddie shook his head. "Jake, the Eagles will double-team you every time you're on the ice. They'll find a way to shut you down."

I looked Freddie square in the eye and answered, "Nobody's shutting me down in this game. You're gonna stop the puck and I'm gonna score. Simple. We will win, Freddie."

Freddie smiled. "You really think we can do it?"

I stood up and grabbed my gear. "We can do it."

I leaned down and pulled on my laces. My legs were jumping so much that I was having trouble tying my skates. As soon as I had them done up, I started pacing back and forth in the dressing room. I had never felt this kind of nervous energy before. I wanted to win this game so badly I could taste it.

Mr. Whitney was busy filling the water bottles when I walked over to him. "How much time, Coach?" I asked.

"'Bout five more minutes," Whitney said. "How do you feel, Jake?"

"I just want to get out there."

"I'm sure you'll be fine. Just play hard."

I paced back to the other end of the dressing room. *Just play hard?* I thought. *Real original advice.*

I sat back down beside Freddie and my legs began to jackhammer up and down. "Oh man, I've got to get out of here."

Freddie didn't answer. He was as white as a ghost.

I looked around at my teammates. Some of the guys were sitting calmly, some were laughing and joking, and I suddenly had this sick feeling that they had already decided we couldn't beat the Eagles.

"Hey, boys!" I yelled out. "Time to focus." Maybe it was because I hardly ever speak in the room, or maybe it was because they really were ready to play, but whatever the reason, everyone went dead quiet.

Just then the door opened and Coach Madigan came in. He was about the same shade of grey as Freddie, and my heart sank. I had never seen him look rattled. Madigan scanned the room and clapped his hands.

"All right, boys, listen up." He tried to smile but it came across more like a gas pain. "The situation's pretty simple. If we win this game, we get to play in the Elite Division of the Quebec Peewee Tournament. If we lose this game, we still get to play in Quebec. My advice to you is to try and enjoy the moment. This is a game that you'll remember for the rest of your lives."

Some of the guys were nodding their heads at Madigan's advice, others had their heads down, and some were so fidgety that they didn't even seem to be listening.

"Freddie," Madigan called. "I want to see you out nice and high; don't stay back in the net. Challenge their shooters and force them to beat you."

Freddie nodded nervously.

"D," Madigan called, and the defencemen all looked up. "Keep their forwards to the outside. Stand up and challenge at our blue line. Let's not make it easy for them to get shots. And forwards, keep it simple. If nothing is there, get the cycle going down low and try to create chances. Remember, lots of shots, just like a playoff game. Throw the puck at the net and look for rebounds. This game could be decided by an ugly goal."

Finally, Madigan looked at me. "Jakey, if I was coaching against you, I'd have two guys on you the whole game. Don't get frustrated if you can't get anything going. You'll have to rely on your teammates. Don't try to do everything by yourself."

"Okay, Coach," I said.

He took a deep breath and smiled. "Well, I guess that's it, boys. Let's go get 'em."

The team jumped up and formed a line behind Freddie. A few guys yelled out some words of encouragement, but most of us were quiet. As we made our way toward the ice surface, I felt the energy. Between our families and the Toronto fans, the rink was hopping. This was what I lived for: a chance to show a rink full of people—and my dad—just how good I could be when the pressure was on.

Okay, I thought. *Let's get this thing started.*

Just as I had expected, the match felt like a playoff game. It was hard-hitting and aggressive. Guys threw themselves fearlessly in front of shots in an effort to prevent the other team from generating any decent scoring chances.

I got very frustrated with the tight checking. As Coach Madigan had predicted, the Eagles double-teamed me and for most of the first period my line was a non-factor. The checking was so intense from both teams that neither side was able to generate many good chances. But late in the first period the Eagles trapped us deep in our own zone. The puck went back to the point and an Eagles' defenceman took a weak shot toward our goal. It was a high floater, and it looked like Freddie saw it all the way, but it waffled over his glove and hit the top corner of the net. It was a softy, but it held up as the game's only goal, and at the end of the first period we found ourselves behind 1–0.

Between periods Coach Madigan told us to keep plugging away. "The breaks will come, boys," he said. Like most of us, now that the action had started he appeared calmer than he had before the game. Then he leaned over the boards and gave Freddie a pat on the shoulder.

"Shake that one off, buddy, and get ready for the next one."

Freddie nodded and headed toward the net just as the referee blew his whistle to get the teams back out to resume play.

The second period was a carbon copy of the first. Each team checked ferociously and at the halfway point of the game, I had yet to muster a shot on net.

After another exasperating shift in which two Eagles players had hit me as soon as the puck came near me, I sat on the bench and cursed under my breath. I grabbed a water bottle and took a gulp, then turned and faced my line mates.

"Guys, this isn't working."

My left winger was a tiny little guy named Lyle Richmond. What Lyle lacked in size he made up for in hockey sense and magic hands. Lyle was a pure goal scorer.

"Jakey, I'm wide open on every shift," he said. "It's like they've decided not to cover me."

"Well, that makes sense," I said. "There's no need to cover you because I can't get you . . ." My voice trailed off as a new thought forced its way into my head.

"What?" Lyle asked.

" . . . the puck. I can't get you the puck."

I turned to my right winger, Joseph Winslow. Joey was a big, strong kid who loved to do the dirty work. He was a mucker and he wore the label proudly. "Joey, listen up. We've got a new game plan."

Joey was more than ready to listen. Whatever I wanted to do would be okay by him.

"We're getting killed because I can't get the puck. Every time I move, they've got two guys on me—"

I was interrupted by a roar from the crowd. All three of us jerked our heads back toward the action just in time to see the Toronto players celebrating in front of Freddie.

"No!" Lyle yelled. "They just scored again."

Joey slammed his stick against the boards and cursed. "This is not good!"

"Jake!" Madigan yelled. "Get out there!"

The three of us stood up and waited for Coach Whitney to open the gate.

"What's the plan, Jake?" Joey asked.

Oh man, I thought. *I need more time.*

I stepped out onto the ice and turned back to face the bench. "Coach," I called. "I need you to call a timeout."

"But Jake, it's only the second period," Madigan protested.

Just then the referee blew his whistle and skated over. "Come on, Coach," he said. "Either take your timeout or take two minutes for delay of game."

I stared at Madigan, willing him to take the timeout. Finally, Coach turned back to the referee and said, "May I have a timeout, please?"

The referee blew his whistle. "Timeout white," he yelled.

We gathered at the bench. "Got an idea, Jake?" Madigan asked.

I nodded. "I can't get open because I'm being double-teamed. This is what I want to do." I turned to Joseph. "Joey, I want you to shadow me."

"Shadow you?"

"Yeah, shadow me," I repeated. "I'm losing puck battles because I'm outnumbered. I need you to help me even the numbers."

Madigan was smiling. "Right on, Jake. I see where you're going. My guess is they'll end up putting a third player on you guys when they make the adjustment."

"Which should open up all kinds of ice for Lyle and the defencemen," I said. "Lyle you need to play like a rover. Wherever Joey and I go, you need to go to the other side of the rink. Don't play like a left winger. Just go to open spots on the ice. We'll find you and get you the puck."

"You got it," Lyle said just as the ref blew his whistle to end the timeout.

I went to centre ice and got ready for the faceoff. *Come on, Jake,* I said to myself. *You need to turn this game around right now.*

The ref dropped the puck and I won the draw back to Sheldon Neely, my right defenceman. Sheldon backpedalled and looked to make a play. I skated over to the right side and stood beside Joey.

"Get ready for some company," I yelled.

Sure enough, two Toronto forwards skated up behind me and tried to pin me against the wall. Sheldon carried the puck and when he hit the red line he was immediately challenged by the Eagles' right winger. He forced Sheldon over to the wall, but this time Joey and I were there waiting for him. A huge scrum followed along the wall as six players fought for possession of the puck. With Joey there to help out, I won my first loose puck of the game. I bolted from the pile and attacked hard at the two remaining Eagles' defenders. Both players converged on me as I skated down the right wall. Just as I was about to be hit, I flipped a soft pass to the left side of the ice. The only player there was Lyle, and he was wide open with a clear-cut breakaway to the net. The last thing I saw before the two Eagles players creamed me into the boards was Lyle putting a beautiful deke on the goalie. The period ended with Toronto up 2–1, but the momentum was clearly starting to swing our way.

Our midgame adjustment had a huge effect. Joey and I were able to out-duel the two Toronto players that were assigned the task of trying to shut me down. Lyle scampered around the ice and gave the rest of the Eagles fits. He seemed to be everywhere. Our line generated several good scoring chances and Toronto suddenly found themselves being very defensive.

Partway through the third period the Eagles made the adjustment we had been waiting for. All three Toronto forwards covered me. This left their two defencemen to cover Lyle and our two "D." Joey and I were paying a huge physical price; we were getting hit and hit hard every time we touched the puck, but that was okay because I knew this game was about to change. It had to.

I sat down on the bench, exhausted. "Joey," I gasped.

Joey was out of gas too. "What, Jake?"

"We're gonna tie this thing up, this shift," I said.

Joey tried to grin but he was too wiped. "Sounds good to me."

"So, don't help me anymore," I said.

Joey's eyes widened. "Don't help you?"

"Yeah, just play right wing."

"But Jake, you've got three guys on you."

I smiled a tired smile. "Exactly."

Realization dawned on Joey. "You got it, Jake!"

Toronto shot the puck on net and Freddie covered it for a whistle. We stood up and headed out for our next shift. The faceoff was to Freddie's right. I won the draw back into the corner for Sheldon, but before he could react, I bolted from the faceoff circle. Instead of heading up ice and looking for a pass, I turned back to the left side of the rink and cut back into the far corner. All three Eagles forwards followed me and Sheldon suddenly had a wide-open path up the ice. By the time the Eagles forwards figured out what had happened, Sheldon, Lyle, and Joey were cutting through the neutral zone. Sheldon hit Lyle with a nice pass, which Lyle took wide on the Eagles' defenceman, then cut hard to the net. He took a low quick shot that the Eagles' goalie kicked back into the middle of the rink. Sheldon grabbed the rebound and hammered another shot at him. Again, the goalie made a nice save, but he couldn't handle the rebound. The puck bounced to the goalie's left, landing right on Joey's stick, and he made no mistake as he banged the loose puck into the back of the net. He let out a whoop and jumped into the air. I was the first player there to greet him, grabbing my big teammate in a bear hug. "Way to go!" I yelled.

Lyle joined the celebration and gave Joey a couple of whacks with his stick.

"We got 'em now, boys," he said.

We skated back to the bench, whooping and yelling the whole way. Madigan met us at the gate and told us to cut it out.

"Save your energy, boys, it's only tied. We need to win in order to pass these guys in the standings. Now settle down, and get ready for your next shift."

I glanced at the clock. Three and a half minutes to go. I knew the Toronto coach would be telling his team that a tie was all they needed to stay in first place. I could almost hear him saying to just calm down and play some defence.

Our other two lines continued to pressure and Toronto continued to struggle and the clock continued to tick toward the end of the game.

With one minute and thirty-seven seconds left, the Toronto goaltender froze the puck after another mad scramble around his net, as several of our guys tried desperately to bang home the winning goal.

"Jake!" Madigan yelled. "I'm gonna pull Freddie. A tie doesn't do us any good."

"Okay, Coach," I said as I headed out for the faceoff, which was to the right of the Eagles' goalie. I watched the linesman's hand. The moment it moved, I moved. I slashed hard at the Toronto centreman's stick and knocked it out of the way. Then I swept the puck back to Sheldon. He hammered a slapshot at the net and every player on the ice attacked the net and looked for the rebound. The goalie bobbled the shot, and the puck bounced loose in front of him. Five defenders desperately tried to clear the puck and six attackers swarmed in to try and knock it into the goal. I stood off to the side of the net and prayed that the puck would pop loose. Sure enough it did, but before I could slam it home, I was tackled to the ice by a desperate Toronto defender. The goalie smothered the puck, and a huge scrum broke out in front of him. The referee blew his whistle repeatedly, trying to restore order. Joey and Lyle were pushing and shoving with a couple of Eagles defenders. I struggled back to my feet and joined in the fray. The player that had tackled me shoved me again and sneered, "You're not going to score, Dumont."

I smiled cockily and was about to say something smart-mouthed, when the Toronto player hauled off and swung a hay-maker that caught me right in the face. The punch snapped my head back and rattled my teeth, but I kept my cool. I knew the kid was trying to goad me into a penalty, and there was no way I was going to spend the end of this game sitting in the box.

"Is that all you've got?" I said. "My mother hits harder than that."

The player swung again, and again my head snapped back.

The referee grabbed the Toronto player and pulled him away from me.

"Let's go, tough guy," he yelled.

The Toronto player looked completely shocked. "What for?" he asked incredulously.

"Two for roughing," the ref answered.

"What about him?" he demanded and pointed menacingly at me.

The ref laughed. "What for? Two minutes for getting punched in the head? Now quit your whining and get in the box."

The Toronto bench erupted in chaos when they realized that they would have to play the final fifty-three seconds short-handed. Their coach called a timeout. We went back to our bench for a breather before the final push on the Toronto goal.

Madigan grabbed his whiteboard and quickly drew up a play. We could hardly hear him because the arena was so loud. The Toronto fans were yelling encouragement to their team while our fans were stomping their feet and banging the backs of their seats. It sounded more like an NHL sellout than a midweek Peewee game. At that moment, as I leaned on the boards trying to catch my breath, I felt an incredible calmness come over me. I looked at Madigan as he was drawing up his play and all the sounds in the arena disappeared. The only thing I could hear was Coach's voice.

"Jake, if you can win the draw, let's set you up on the left half board and we'll try to make a back-door pass to Lyle." He pointed to the right of the net where he wanted Lyle to stand. Everybody knew how much was riding on my next faceoff.

I glanced at my teammates and I saw something that I was

all too familiar with. I saw their fear. "Hey, guys," I called out, just as the referee blew his whistle to end the timeout. "We got this. I'm gonna win the draw and Lyle's gonna bang one home. Now let's go break their hearts."

Joey laughed and gave me a smack on the shin pads with his stick. "I like it!" he yelled. "Come on, boys, let's go break some hearts."

We skated back to the faceoff dot and I willed myself to win another draw. The linesman dropped the puck and the Toronto centreman and I battled for it. Suddenly, the puck popped loose and Lyle grabbed it and sent a pass back to Sheldon. He didn't have a clear shooting lane so he pulled the puck across the blue line and tried to set up a play. I positioned myself on the left half wall, and for the first time all game, I found myself without someone covering me. Sheldon saw me and fed me a nice pass. I took the puck and immediately looked for Lyle. The Toronto defenders all shifted across the ice to my side, trying to block my path to the net and my path back to Sheldon. For a moment, I could see Lyle wide open, standing behind the Toronto coverage. I whipped a pass back across the rink, and Lyle one-timed the pass at the net. The Toronto goalie made an incredible save, and the puck bounced crazily into the corner. I watched as Joey chased a Toronto defender and hammered him into the boards just as he was about to clear the puck out of the zone. The puck came weakly around the boards to me, and I pulled it off the boards and stepped to the top of the faceoff circle. Without thinking, I took a deep breath and unleashed a slapshot. I watched the puck as it rifled toward the top corner of the net. In a bizarre replay of our earlier game, the puck ricocheted off the crossbar and a loud *ping* echoed through the rink. Then I saw Lyle at the corner of the net jumping up and down like crazy, and suddenly, Joey tackled me to the ice, followed by Sheldon and the rest of the team. When the boys finally let me up, I looked at Lyle and laughed.

"Crossbar and in?" I asked.

Lyle nodded and grinned. "Crossbar and in, baby! Goalie never had a chance!"

The referee dropped the puck and the final three seconds ticked off the clock. We swarmed Freddie and a huge celebration erupted in his goal crease.

Back in the dressing room, we let out a big cheer when Coach Madigan asked, "How's it feel to be in first place, boys?" He beamed. "Well, I guess we'll go to Quebec and see what the rest of the hockey world has to offer. Congratulations, I'm really proud of you."

We yelled and screamed and carried on as if we had just won the Stanley Cup. Eventually, we quieted down, changed, and headed out of the room. As usual, the last two players to leave the room were me and Freddie. We were lingering there, basking in the glow of victory, when Madigan came back to collect the jerseys. He still had an enormous grin on his face.

"Great game, Freddie," he said.

"Thanks, Coach."

"And Jake?" I stood up and shouldered my hockey bag. "I told you it would go in when we needed it to."

"You sure did, Coach." I laughed.

He walked me out of the dressing room, giving my hair a scruff. "That was an incredible shot, kid," he said. "Now go on home and enjoy the win."

CHAPTER EIGHT

I tried to walk calmly out of the arena, but I was so excited about my goal and our big win that I was practically hopping down the hallway. The first person I saw as I came into the lobby was my mom. She wrapped her arms around me and gave me a big hug. "I'm so proud of you," she whispered into my ear.

"Thanks, Mom" I said. "Where's Dad?"

"He went out to warm up the van. Are you ready to go?"

Mom chatted away excitedly as we walked across the parking lot in the cold night air. We were just about to the van when I saw Dad get out and walk to the back. He lifted up the tailgate and reached for my sticks.

"Nice shot," he said, as he threw them in.

"Thanks!" I said. For the first time in a long time, he seemed to be in a good mood after a game.

But then he put his hand on his forehead and slid his fingers through his hair, then yanked my hockey bag from my shoulder and heaved it into the van. He slammed the tailgate down hard, and then he spun around to face me. Even in the darkness I could tell that he was shaking.

"A goal and an assist in a huge game like that—" He paused. "Well, I guess that's something."

I felt like a balloon that was leaking air. My good mood, the excitement of the game, and my goal were seeping out of me.

"What do you mean, 'something'?" I asked.

"Well, you played a good game, for sure," he said. "But sometimes it's like you just don't get it."

I didn't get it and answered honestly, "Get what?"

"Get what?" he answered incredulously. "A kid punched you in the face and you did nothing about it."

"Yes I did!" I challenged. "I scored the winning goal!"

Dad rolled his eyes. "Yeah, yeah, you scored the winning goal and that's good, but scouts don't care about that. They care about toughness. You should have fought that kid and showed everyone what you're made of."

I looked at Mom in disbelief. She shook her head ever so slightly, but I was too angry to heed her warning. I had a sudden vision of the other guys on my team. I was thinking about Lyle and Joey and the way their dads would react if one of them had scored the winning goal. There would be hugs and high-fives and backslapping. There would be pride. But for me there was no pride, just my dad angrily running his hand through his hair. Rage that I had suppressed for years rushed to the surface and threatened to boil over.

I turned on Dad and growled, "Toughness? I scored the winning goal in the biggest game of my life, and you're worried about toughness!"

"Don't take that tone with me, boy," he warned.

"Don't, Jake," Mom said. "Just don't say another word." She put her hand on my back and tried to move between me and Dad. "Jeff," she said shakily. "Please, let's not make a scene."

Dad took a deep breath, then slowly nodded. "I was just trying to help Jake out. Make him into the best player that he can be. And in my opinion, scouts are looking for toughness."

"Okay," Mom agreed. "But can we maybe talk about this at home where we won't be, I don't know, bothering anyone?"

Dad took another breath, put his hand on my shoulder and gave it a squeeze. "Sure, we'll talk about it at home," he agreed, steering me toward the back seat of the van.

Maybe it was because I was so pumped up about the win and the goal, only to have my dad wreck my night, but whatever the reason, I just couldn't let it go.

"What do you know about getting scouted?" I challenged. "Were you ever scouted?"

Dad stopped dead.

I looked up into his face. "Well, were ya?"

"No, I wasn't," he said quietly.

"Is that because you were psycho, or because you just plain sucked?"

It took a second for that to sink in, but when it did his face clouded with anger. I think he would have decked me right on the spot, but another voice cut through the night and stopped him cold.

"Good night, Dumonts!"

Dad's eyes searched for the voice. I turned around to see Coach Madigan shuffling past with the team jerseys, water bottles, and his briefcase.

"Hey, Coach," I called out. "You need a hand?"

"No, I'm good, Jake," he called back. "Go on home and enjoy the win. Your boy played a heck of a game, Jeff!" Madigan yelled happily, as he continued toward his car.

"Thanks, Coach," Dad answered evenly.

My heart sank as I watched Madigan disappear into the darkness.

"You heard the man, Jake," Dad hissed quietly over my shoulder. "Let's go home and enjoy the win."

We drove home in silence. Dad didn't even put the radio on to listen to his sports channels. The seat belt that was supposed to be keeping me safe felt more like a straitjacket, and the van was my own personal little prison. I guess that I'd always known that my home life was screwed up, but tonight something was changing. I had always seen Dad as someone to be feared. Someone I tried to avoid. Someone I tried not to upset. But tonight, new feelings were slamming around inside me. I was sad and scared and upset, but mostly I was *angry*—angry that he'd ruined my night. I was proud of my team, proud of my goal, proud of myself, and he had to ruin it. Muttered some crap about scouts and toughness. We had just qualified for the Quebec Peewee Tournament and that still wasn't good enough. The more I thought about it, the madder I got.

As we pulled into the driveway, I realized that for the first time in my life I didn't care how my dad was going to react. He had already reacted in his weird way and had tried to show me who was the boss. Was this all just some bizarre head game for him? Well, tonight I wouldn't play the game. The anger was my shield, and I was ready for battle.

I got out of the van and pulled my gear from the tailgate. Dad appeared beside me and said, "We'll talk inside."

I lifted my hockey bag up onto my shoulder, grabbed the tailgate, and pulled it closed. Then I looked him in the eye. "Whatever," I answered. I pushed past him and started up the walk.

He grabbed me by the arm and spun me around. "You get to your room right now," he said.

Again, I looked him in the eye. "Actually, the first thing I have to do is go to the basement and hang up my gear. Then I'm going to have a shower, and then I have homework. So why don't you just leave me alone. I've got things to do." Before he could respond, I yanked my arm free and headed for the door. I was half expecting a smack to the back of the head, but instead, I heard him complain to Mom.

"You see how he treats me, Rebecca? No respect."

"He's just upset, Jeff," Mom answered cautiously. "It was a big night for him, and he was so excited."

I couldn't hear what else she said because I was already at the garage door. I threw it open and headed for the basement.

After I hung up my gear, I went to the bathroom. I was thinking about the confrontation that was still to come tonight. No question it was going to hurt, and part of me felt that the easiest thing to do would be to just get it over with. I was so absorbed in my own thoughts that I almost missed it.

"He thinks he knows everything, but he doesn't. He could make the NHL if he'd just shut up and listen to me."

It was Dad's voice, coming through the air vent from my parents' bedroom.

"Jeff, he's just a little boy," Mom tried to reason.

"He's a little boy who's going to learn to respect his father. You heard the way he spoke to me."

"He was upset," Mom answered. "It was such a big night for him, scoring the—"

That's strange, I thought. Why'd she stop talking?

Dad's voice again: "I am so sick and tired of you defending him."

The house was eerily quiet for a moment before the sound of a sob came through the vent.

With a sick feeling, I stormed out of the bathroom and walked purposefully down the hall. I think I'd always known that Dad hurt my mom too, even though I'd never actually seen it. Maybe she was just as good at hiding things as I was. As I pulled open their bedroom door I knew that the days of hiding and pretending were about to come to an end.

Mom was sitting on the bed, holding her ear with her left hand. Dad was standing over her. He spun around and glared at me.

"How dare you come into our room without knocking."

"Get your hands off her," I demanded.

"It's okay, Jake. Everything's fine," Mom said shakily.

"It's not fine," I said, moving toward them.

The punch came hard and fast, and even though I had been expecting it, it still sent me sprawling backwards. A jolt of pain went searing through my face. Dad's fist was big enough that the punch made contact with my eye, my cheek, and my jaw. My teeth slammed together and the whole side of my face began to throb. Already, I could feel my eye beginning to close.

Willing myself not to cry, I pushed myself back up and stood as straight as I could.

Mom was trying to grab hold of Dad, but he effortlessly shoved her onto the bed.

"I said don't touch her!" I shouted. I was trying to think of something else to say when he swung at me with an open hand and caught me hard across the left cheek.

My head snapped back, but this time I stayed on my feet. I turned my face back toward him and slowly I raised my fists and held them out in front of me like a boxer. I willed myself to speak clearly.

"That is the last time you will ever hit me," I said.

To my surprise, Dad smiled. "There you go," he said. "That's what I've been talking about. Fight back. That's the toughness that I want to see. You're finally starting to get it. Now, why don't you grab that shower and then get your homework done. I'm gonna go and watch the Leafs game." And with that he pushed past me and walked out of the room.

CHAPTER NINE

I paced around my room and tried to calm myself down. I'd never been in a fight before. Sure I'd been beaten up lots of times, but tonight was different. Tonight I had fought back, or at least stood up for myself. My hands were still shaking and I was still really mad at my dad.

You should have fought to show the scouts how tough you are.

Give me a break, I thought. *You want tough? Try getting beaten up every time your dad thinks you didn't play well enough.* I ran over to my trophy shelf, grabbed a large one, and threw it as hard as I could. It smashed off the wall and busted in half. I stood panting in the middle of the room, years of rage coursing through my body. My door opened and my mom slipped into my room.

"Are you okay?" she asked.

"Am I okay?" I asked incredulously. "Do I look okay?"

She looked at my eye, which by now was completely closed,

and sighed. "Jake, your father, he just wants what's best for you—"

I cut her off. "Are you serious?"

"Jake, listen to me—"

"No, you listen to *me*," I interrupted. "He's crazy, and we need to get out of here—now!"

"Jake you need to be reasonable. I know that you're upset, but you need to calm down. Everything will be better in the morning."

"Mom, I'm not safe here," I said, pointing at my eye. "And you aren't either." I pointed at her ear. "We need to go."

Mom sighed. "Where would we go?"

"I don't care. Anywhere. But we need to go *now*."

"Jake," Mom said, "if you would just try to do what he wants…"

I stared at her, disbelieving. "What did you say?"

"It's just that if you could just try to please him once in a while and not argue with him." I think she would have said more, but she stopped when she saw the look on my face.

"You know what, Mom? Forget it. Don't worry about it. I'll talk to you in the morning."

She smiled sadly. "Things will be better tomorrow, you'll see."

After she left, I flopped on my bed and tried to collect my thoughts. Something had changed tonight. In my anger I had convinced myself that I wasn't scared anymore. But now I realized that I wasn't just scared, I was terrified. My dad wasn't safe to be around. My mom was the only person who knew what I was going through, and she was defending him. I was worried about her and wanted to protect her, but I also needed to protect myself. I tried to clear my head so that I could assess my options.

If I showed up at school in the morning with another shiner, there would be no way to explain this one away. Mr. Hamilton was a nice guy and I knew that he'd want to help, but what could he do? Call the principal? Call the police? Call my mom? My stomach flipped just thinking about that.

I could take off tonight and sneak over to Freddie's place. He'd hide me for the night, but I knew that eventually I'd still end up back home. Everything I thought of ended with me being back at home with nothing changing. Finally, I decided what I needed to do.

I went to my closet and rummaged around the top shelf until I found my backpack. I unzipped the main panel and peeked inside. It contained several water bottles, a handful of granola bars, mitts, a toque, a large sweatshirt, a pocketknife, a flashlight, a map of the Toronto subway system, and several dollars in loose change. I went to my desk and got out my birthday and Christmas money. Taking a piece of paper from my school binder, I sat down and wrote a note to my mom.

Dear Mom,

I'm sorry to do this to you, but I can't live in the same house as Dad anymore. Don't worry about me, I can look after myself. I hope that you will be able to look after your-self too. Tell Coach Madigan that I'm sorry and I feel bad about letting the team down. I'd love to play in the Quebec Tournament, but it's just not worth it.

Love, Jake

I reread the letter several times, then sat on my bed and waited impatiently for my clock radio to show 1 a.m. I was far too nervous to fall asleep, and I spent the time trying to come up with a more concrete plan. I knew I needed to leave, but I had no idea where I was going.

Finally, it was time to get dressed. I put on a pair of long underwear, jeans, a turtleneck, and a thick sweater. I grabbed another turtleneck and several pairs of socks and did my best to cram them into my already overstuffed backpack. When I was sure that I hadn't forgotten anything I quietly opened the door. It was time to go.

PART TWO

CHAPTER TEN

I ran toward the entrance of the subway and flew down the steps two at a time. I was reaching into my pocket to pull out some loose change for the fare when an elderly man in a TTC uniform came out of the kiosk, closing the door behind him. He caught sight of me.

I suddenly felt nervous. "How much for a fare?" I asked politely.

The old man smiled kindly. "Oh, I'm sorry. The subway's closed for the night."

He seemed to detect my panic as I digested this information. He was also eyeing the massive goose egg covering my eye.

"Are you okay?" he asked. "Would you like me to call you a cab?"

I shook my head.

"Call your folks?"

I looked down at the floor. "That's okay," I mumbled.

The man smiled conspiratorially. "Tell you what. There's a Tim Hortons just around the corner. Why don't you grab yourself a bite to eat and warm up a bit. In a little while you can come back here. Nobody will bother you and you'll be able to stay warm until morning. The subway starts running again at six."

"Thanks for your help," I said.

"You just make sure you take care of yourself."

I tried to smile. "I'll do my best."

Then I ran back up the stairs and into the night.

I had eaten at Timmy's thousands of times and had never batted an eye at the price. Now that I thought about it, I couldn't remember ever having to pay. My parents had always done that. I had never really thought too much about how much a doughnut and a drink cost, but as I sat there chewing, I ran the numbers in my head. My money wasn't going to last very long if I had to buy all my meals. Running away was a crazy idea. I took a sip from my drink and surveyed my surroundings. I wasn't entirely sure that the old man at the subway hadn't gone and called the police as soon as he was finished talking to me. I didn't like the thought of being trapped in Tim Hortons by the police. I shuddered at the embarrassment of being returned to my house in the middle of the night by a cop.

I glanced at my watch: 2:55. I had been on the run now for just over an hour and a half. I was enjoying the warmth of the restaurant, but I worried about staying in one place for too long. I also knew that a young kid with a giant shiner sitting alone at three in the morning would stand out in people's memories. I grudgingly stood up, drained the rest of my pop, and headed back out into the cold night. I walked briskly back toward the subway station. As I got closer, I slowed my pace and looked around cautiously in case the police were lurking in the darkness, just waiting to pounce on me.

About ten metres from the subway entrance, a large maple tree provided some shelter from the glare of the street lights. I bent over, pretending to tie up my boot. Slowly I shuffled around until I was hidden on the shaded side of the tree. Then I waited in the darkness while I studied my surroundings. I scanned the street for police officers, but it was absolutely quiet. The entire city of North York appeared to be sleeping.

When I was sure that I was the only person in the area that was still awake, I made a dash for the stairway. I felt dangerously exposed under the bright street lights, and I was sure that I'd never reach the stairs undetected. I hit the top stair and bolted down. My footfalls echoed loudly off the walls, and I panicked thinking that the noise would awaken the entire neighbourhood. Inside the station, I tried the handle to the kiosk door, but wasn't surprised to find it locked. A row of turnstiles blocked my way toward another tunnel that led down to the subway platform. I sprinted toward the nearest one, leapfrogged it easily, and landed on the other side. I covered the foyer in a few quick strides and pounded down another flight of stairs, landing at the bottom with a thud, then stopped. The tunnel was completely black. I couldn't see a thing. My first instinct was to turn around and run back up toward the welcoming glow of light, but I willed myself to calm down. The darkness was my friend; it would hide me.

My eyes began to adjust to the darkness. The platform wasn't quite as dark as down on the tracks where the trains ran. Ahead of me, about five metres away, I could make out the silhouette of a large pillar in the middle of the platform. Summoning all my courage, I began to shuffle forward with my hands out in front of me. I reached the pillar and groped my way around it until I was on the far side from the stairs. Maybe it would block me from view if anyone should come searching for me.

I took off my backpack and sat leaning against the pillar. I figured I would be able to stay awake the few short hours until the subway reopened, but within a few minutes, my eyes felt heavy and my head began to droop forward. I pulled my backpack in tight beside me and flopped over on my side. With the pillar as a makeshift barrier and the backpack as a pillow, I fell into a deep sleep.

Voices jolted me awake. For a second I didn't know where I was. Then memory came rushing back, and I was gripped by fear. They were looking for me! I scrambled back up to a crouching position and tried to hide behind the pillar. Clutching my backpack to my chest, I held my breath and waited.

Footfalls on the stairs! People were coming, and I was trapped. I cowered against the pillar, unable to move, until two men in business suits walked past me. One looked my way, then quickly diverted his eyes. The other didn't even notice me. More voices, more footfalls. The overhead lights slowly brightened as if they, too, were having difficulty waking up from their long night's sleep. The platform was coming to life with the morning's commuters.

Relieved, I rubbed my arms vigorously, then stood up and tried to stretch out the kinks in my back. I was still worried about drawing attention to myself, but as I looked around the platform I could see that nobody cared whether or not a homeless kid slept on the platform for the night. They were too busy to worry about me. A few minutes later, a large roar filled the tunnel as the first train of the day came rocketing into view. It screeched to a stop, the doors opened, and the commuters boarded. I shouldered my backpack and followed the crowd heading downtown.

Once seated, I studied the subway map above the train doors. I had boarded at Leslie Street and was heading west. In order to get to downtown Toronto, I would need to transfer onto the Yonge Street line and take the southbound train. Each time we pulled into a station I would read the name on the wall and double-check the map above the doors. After leaving the Bayview Station, one stop before Yonge, I walked over to the doors so I'd be sure to have enough time to get off. When they hissed open a few minutes later, I stepped out and joined a sea of people. The fast walkers darted around slower ones. Experienced commuters barely broke stride as they swiped their cards, slammed the turnstiles with their hips, and hurried toward their trains.

I felt overwhelmed as I tried to navigate my way through the crowd. A bench snaked along one wall and I worked my way over to it and sat down. For the first time in my life I wasn't on any sort of schedule—no hockey, no school. I dug through my backpack and pulled out a granola bar and a water bottle. As I munched on my breakfast, I watched the commuters from all walks of life flow past me: male, female, short, tall, rich, poor, fat, skinny, young, old, black, white, and every shade in between. It would be really easy to disappear into the crowd. When I was finished eating, I repacked all of my worldly goods. Then I found a men's room and washed up.

I went to the ticket kiosk and reluctantly paid the fare; I was worrying about money again. When the next train arrived, I crowded onto it with no idea where I was going or what I was going to do once I got there.

As the subway worked its way closer to downtown Toronto, I tried to formulate a plan. The problem of finding shelter for tonight was beginning to frighten me. I supposed that I could sleep in another subway terminal, but I worried about getting caught and I worried about freezing. It was almost Christmas and the temperature seemed to drop a little more each day.

I chose to get off at the only street name I recognized— Dundas. I'd been to the Eaton Centre at Yonge and Dundas with my mom and figured the gigantic mall was as good a place as any to start looking for a place to sleep.

For a while I just walked around Dundas Square and took in the sights and sounds. Christmas carols seemed to be coming from every storefront. Giant LCD screens were mounted on the sides of buildings. They played movie ads and told the pedestrians walking by on the streets below what they should be watching on TV that night. Street musicians stood beside their open guitar cases and played festive tunes in an effort to coax some loose change from the pockets of passersby. One man was drawing on the sidewalk. He had blocked off a large section with pylons and everyone obligingly walked around the Picasso wannabe. Some stopped to watch the work in progress and some even threw coins into a bucket that was placed at the bottom of the picture.

I watched the man work and laughed to myself when I saw that he was using a child's set of sidewalk chalk. Then I took a closer look and stopped laughing. It was the picture of Muhammad Ali standing defiantly over a fallen Sonny Liston. What caught my attention was the expression on Ali's face. The artist had captured a look of rage mixed with pure euphoria. The drawing was incredible, and I stayed and watched the artist work for the longest time. When my feet started to get cold, I decided to move on. I wanted to leave the guy some money, but I needed to guard every penny. Feeling slightly guilty, I blended back into the crowd.

The Eaton Centre was on my left and I thought about heading inside. I could wander for hours without attracting any attention, and I would be warm. But I wanted to explore my new surroundings. Now that I knew where the mall was, I could come back anytime if I couldn't find a better spot for shelter. I decided to head north on Yonge Street and meandered slowly, weaving my way in and out of the crowd. Eventually, as I waited for a green light at a corner, I spied a pizza joint. My stomach growled angrily. The only food that I had eaten since last night was a doughnut and a granola bar. My brain tried to reason with my stomach.

Food costs money! We need to save it!

My stomach growled louder in response. The light turned green, and my legs, not knowing whether to side with my stomach or my brain, hesitated. In the end, my brain won the argument, and I continued up the street.

The atmosphere on this part of the street was completely different. I was entering a scarier part of town. Storefront windows displayed T-shirts with rude sayings and various types of drug-related merchandise. Tired, worn-out men loitered on the sidewalk outside the stores. They seemed to have nowhere to go and nothing to do. I lowered my eyes and walked quickly past. Half a block farther north I noticed a soup kitchen. How many of the men that I had just passed were waiting for it to open?

At the next intersection I spied another Tim Hortons. *Man, they're everywhere,* I thought, as my stomach growled even more loudly than before. *Okay, okay, relax. We'll go and get some food.*

Standing in line, I figured I should try to eat something healthy, so I ordered a soup and sandwich combo. I resisted the urge to order a pop and asked the lady for milk. Reluctantly, I parted with my money and found a seat. I was learning to move slowly whenever I was in a warm place. I savoured every mouthful of my soup, then polished off the sandwich and milk.

Back outside, I took a look around to reorient myself. I checked the name of the cross street as I waited for the light. Carlton Street.

Something in the deep reaches of my memory stirred. I recognized that name. The crowd of pedestrians surged past me, but I held back and tried to remember. Instead of continuing north, I turned right and began to explore along Carlton. I had only gone a short distance when I noticed an imposing brown building ahead and to my left. Memories began to fire quickly. The image of a large, friendly polar-bear mascot jumped to mind.

Carlton.

Carlton the Bear.
The Toronto Maple Leafs Mascot.
He was named for Carlton Street.

I stopped in front of the building and stared. It dominated over half a city block and seemed to be almost as tall as it was wide. Its brick facing was worn and definitely looked the worse for wear. Decades of car exhaust and air pollution clung to the once-majestic brown brick. It looked like it was in need of a good bath. But it was still the most famous building in the entire hockey world. And to me, Maple Leaf Gardens still looked absolutely beautiful.

CHAPTER ELEVEN

Thousands of Leafs fans had once poured through the glass doors along the front of the arena. Now the doors were covered with paper, preventing people from looking inside. I glanced over my shoulder to see if anyone was watching, then I walked over to the first door and casually pulled on the handle.

Locked.

I moved along and tried each door even though I knew that I wasn't going to have any success. It was getting late, and both the sun and the temperature were beginning to drop. I would need to head back to the Eaton Centre soon and look for a place to spend the night. But I had a strong urge to see inside the Gardens.

I walked to the corner and peeked around it. The arena stretched north a full city block. I walked slowly and admired the rock facing that decorated the lower section of the arena wall. There was another set of glass doors at the far end of the wall.

There were also several small openings that looked like laundry chutes. The doors were all locked and I wasn't sure that I'd be able to squeeze through a chute, even if I could get one of them open.

The arena ended at Wood Street, where I turned left and followed the perimeter of the building. This side of the building was shorter and I was already beginning to form a picture in my mind's eye of the layout inside. This was one of the ends of the rink. My suspicion was confirmed when I noticed a large garage-style door at the back of the arena. It was easily big enough to move a Zamboni through. I tried to force the door open, but again, I came up empty.

It was time to abandon my search and begin the long, cold walk back to the Eaton Centre. The arena sat beside a large hotel that I had not even noticed when I first walked across Carlton Street. Now I saw that a narrow alleyway separated the two buildings. The entrance to the alleyway was blocked by a rusty old metal gate. I looked down the gap between the two buildings. It wasn't more than a couple of metres wide. Old boxes and garbage cluttered the length of it. With the sun setting, the alley was cast in ominous shadow. I walked over to the gate and inspected it. A thick, rusty chain secured by an old lock held it in place. I picked up the lock and examined it—the gate wasn't really locked at all! Someone had wound the chain around it and carefully positioned the lock at the front. Anyone walking by would assume that it was closed up tight.

I took a quick look up and down the street. When I was sure that I wasn't being watched, I unwound the chain and opened the gate. Stepping into the alley, I pulled the gate shut behind me, careful to leave the chain just as I had found it. Then I turned and shuffled a few steps.

I wasn't sure what I was doing or what I was looking for. As I worked my way cautiously down the alley it became harder and harder to see. I removed my backpack and felt inside for my flashlight. It cast a comforting glow all around me as I shone it back and forth on the side of the Gardens. This back wall was a soot-coloured mess. Almost eighty years of air pollution caked the brickwork.

Man, what a dump, I thought.

I was about to head back to the gate when another one of those odd chute-things caught my eye. I bent down and pulled on the handle. To my surprise, the handle moved, and the chute popped open.

I shone my light into the opening and saw a small storage room full of old arena seats and piles of garbage bags. I wondered if I could squeeze through the opening and climb down on the backs of the seats, which were stacked against the wall. Before I could talk myself out of it, I ducked my head through the chute, braced myself on the old seats, and dropped down into the room. I stepped around the debris and, gathering my courage, opened the storage room door.

I was standing in a long, dark hallway.

I'm not scared, I told myself, a little unconvincingly. Then I turned down the hall and moved deeper and deeper into the heart of Maple Leaf Gardens.

CHAPTER TWELVE

I took a moment to try and draw myself a mental map of my surroundings. I was pretty sure that the ice surface was somewhere off to my left. Up ahead, a long way away, I saw a slight glow of light, and I instinctively headed for it. As I worked my way along, the old hallway began to reveal its secrets under the probing glare of my flashlight. Behind an old concession stand was a large billboard-sized advertisement for a 1999 Ford Grand Marquis.

I passed a narrow escalator, which used to take spectators to the upper seats of the Gardens. I made a mental note to come back and examine it in the daylight. As I continued to move forward, I couldn't shake the feeling that I should be more scared. After all, I was snooping around an old, derelict building. But for some reason I was starting to feel calm for the first time since I'd left home. The building smelled old and stale, and it was creepy, but it felt like where I needed to be.

My biggest discovery of the day was yet to come. I was still moving toward the glow of light at the end of the hall when my flashlight illuminated a large opening in the wall to my right. My curiosity peaked; I walked through it and found a large washroom typical of most stadiums. Urinals lined one long wall, a series of toilet stalls lined the other. The room smelled hideous and I resisted the urge to gag and bolt from it. Instead, I held my breath and walked over to the sinks.

Come on, please.

I turned the tap and was greeted by a jet of water.

"Yes!" I yelled triumphantly.

I scooted over to the urinals and flushed one. It worked too. I grinned and ran over to flush a toilet, watching excitedly as the water swirled down the bowl.

Toilet paper! I flashed the light around the stall and, sure enough, there was a roll of toilet paper hanging dutifully in its place. I had no idea why the water would still be working in an abandoned building, but I wasn't going to look a gift horse in the mouth. Now I had shelter, fresh water, and bathroom facilities. All I needed to do was figure out how to feed myself.

Exiting the washrooms, I resumed my journey toward the glowing light. When I got a little closer, I saw what it was. The streetlights on Carlton Street were shining through the paper taped inside the front entrance of the arena. There was enough light here that I was able to turn off my flashlight and preserve the batteries. As I walked slowly along the front of the building, I felt like an archaeologist who had just discovered a long-lost historical site. I marvelled at the murals on the wall showing the great Leafs players from years past. The box office was on my right, and I tried to imagine how busy this hallway must have been on game nights as people bought tickets, hot dogs, and programs before going to their seats.

A large Toronto Maple Leafs logo covered the floor in front of the main doors along Carlton Street. To the side of the logo was a large, rectangular archway. It was a welcome sight. Every arena had them, and I knew that it was the entrance to the ice surface. This one just happened to be a lot bigger than the ones I was used to when I took to the ice with my team.

Leaving the lights behind me, I plunged into the darkness of the archway. I flicked my flashlight back on and saw that I was only a metre or two away from the ice surface. The boards had long since been removed, so I just stepped out onto the floor.

"I'm standing on the floor of Maple Leaf Gardens," I marvelled.

Awestruck, I zipped the flashlight around, not sure what I should look at first, and ended up having a hard time seeing much of anything. It reminded me of a video that Mr. Hamilton had shown the class once about the underwater exploration of the *Titanic*. The lights from the submarine could only illuminate a tiny section of the great ship, so you were left more confused than enlightened by what you were seeing.

Oh well, I thought. *I'll explore more in the morning and hopefully I'll be able to see more.*

I swept the light one last time up the side of the rink and was saddened to see that all the seats had been removed. What had once been a magnificent building was now a tired-looking shell. I aimed my beam up and it bounced off one of the giant silver lights that hung from the arena ceiling. Up at the very top of the Gardens, my light caught a long row of windows that ran the length of the rink. I felt a cold shiver run down my spine. *Someone's up there!* I brought the light back and held it in place.

Nothing.

I played the light back and forth for a few seconds while I tried to calm myself down. *Get a grip, Jake. There's no one up there.*

I dropped the beam and headed back to the archway. I told myself that I wasn't scared, but walked quickly toward the friendly glow of the Carlton Street lights. Back in the main concourse, I looked down at my watch. It was only 6:30. I'd thought it was a lot later than that because of how dark it was. I tried to take my mind off whether or not I had really seen someone up in that window by thinking about what I would do for the rest of the night. As if it was trying to suggest an activity, my stomach let out a growl.

I looked around for a comfortable spot. I walked over to the box office, pulled off my backpack, and sat down. My dinner, like my breakfast, was a granola bar and water. Now that I knew there was a Tim Hortons nearby, I considered walking over to get a proper meal. But what if I couldn't find my storage room at the other end of the Gardens? Besides, I didn't want to go back out into the cold night air. Not to mention, I was exhausted. I'd only had two hours sleep the night before and had been on my feet since 6 a.m.

I pulled out my sweatshirt and my turtleneck and tried to make a cushion on the floor, but it was rock hard and my backpack was a lousy pillow. I was beginning to feel really sorry for myself. I wondered if Mom was okay.

To take my mind off my troubles, I made a list of things that I needed. Some sort of padding for a bed would be nice, and I could really use a sleeping bag.

In spite of my loneliness and discomfort, I soon felt my eyes getting heavy. As I shifted around trying to get comfortable, I suddenly thought about Samantha.

What would Sam think of the mess I've gotten myself into?

Imagining being chastised by Sam, scolded by Sam, or fussed over by Sam made me smile. We had been friends since kindergarten, but I was pretty sure that my current thoughts weren't of the "friendship" variety. "Good night, Sam," I said and closed my eyes.

CHAPTER THIRTEEN

I was suspended in that peaceful world between sleeping and waking. Surfacing from a sound sleep, I resisted opening my eyes for as long as I could. When I did, I was staring up at a bizarre-looking mural of a bunch of guys in Toronto Maple Leafs uniforms. I tried to pull my blankets up, but instead of my duvet curling around me, my sweatshirt bunched up against my face.

I pushed myself up and cried out in pain. Every muscle in my body had stiffened up during the night. My neck felt locked in place, and I had to rub it a long time to straighten it. I attempted to stand up, but my legs weren't too thrilled by this proposition. Eventually, I made it to my feet, and I bent down and tried to touch my toes. I could feel my body slowly loosening up. I put my hands on my hips, did a few trunk rotations, and decided I might actually survive.

"Fresh as a daisy," I muttered.

I walked slowly around the main concourse and the stiffness

began to subside. And now another bodily function needed my attention: I had to pee. The hallway to the washroom was a lot darker than where I had spent the night. I found my flashlight and then looked at my other belongings spread out on the floor. Everything I owned was here. Instinct told me to take my stuff with me, so even though my bladder was beginning to hurt, I carefully repacked my bag. When I was sure that I had everything, I shouldered my bag and walked down the dark hallway.

I sat on the concrete floor where centre ice used to be, and munched my final granola bar. In the daylight, the Gardens revealed a lot more of her secrets. I tried imagining what it must have been like to watch a game here back in the glory days. But my mind kept stubbornly coming back to the here and now. I had just finished the last granola bar and bottle of water. If I ate three meals a day at fast-food places, my money would run out in just over two more days.

I considered my options:

If I cut my meals to once a day, my money would still only last for about eight days. I needed more cash, or I would be forced to go home with my tail between my legs. In the washroom that morning I had looked into a dirty, old mirror. I wiped my arm across it to remove a layer of dirt and grime, and the image that had looked back scared me. The whole left side of my face was bruised and my eye was still swollen. Seeing how my face looked, and knowing that my dad had caused it, was enough to fuel my resolve. I wasn't going home. There had to be another way.

Maybe I can get a job, I thought.

I was wondering about the odds of anyone hiring me with my face looking like it had been run over when the feeling that I was being watched came over me again. I turned my head and peered over my shoulder. The west side of the Gardens towered above me. A bit of light seeped through the archways, but for the most part, that side of the building was blanketed in a hazy veil of semi-darkness. I felt around for my flashlight. In one quick motion I pulled it up, aimed it at the wall, and flicked the switch. I swung the beam of light up and down the length of the building. I didn't see anything, but I couldn't shake the sensation that someone was there. I was short of breath, and my hand shook as it held the flashlight.

I grabbed my backpack and walked toward the Church Street side of the rink, willing myself to move slowly, like I didn't have a care in the world. Heading down a hallway, I passed a room I thought might have been the Leafs' dressing room. Under different circumstances, I would have been thrilled to take my time and do some exploring, but that would have to wait. I popped out into the Church Street concourse and broke into a dead run, racing toward the Carlton Street end of the rink. When I reached the corner of the two main hallways I stopped at a set of paper-covered glass doors. In front of them was a large pile of refuse. Garbage bags, old pieces of ductwork, and mounds of discarded lumber formed a pile two or three metres high.

I dashed in behind the garbage pile and squeezed as close to the doors as I could get. If things went wrong, I would bolt through the doors and not look back. From my hiding spot I could see across the width of the Carlton Street lobby and down the length of the Church Street hallway. I sat there for what seemed like an eternity and tried to control my breathing. I was beginning to feel really silly. After all, I wasn't even sure that there was anyone else in the building. It was probably just my imagination. I was about to stand up when I noticed a flicker of shadow near the box office. My heart jumped into my throat.

Silently, I reached up and put my hand on the door handle. My blood was pounding so loudly in my ears that I was sure that the noise would give away my position. There it was again! The shadow moved slowly along the wall. It moved past the giant Leafs logo on the floor and stopped. Whatever it was, or whoever it was, was moving very slowly and cautiously.

He's looking for me, I thought.

I resisted the urge to go hurtling through the door and run all the way back to North York, and instead, tried to focus my eyes on the shadow.

There!

It moved again and was coming right at me. I held my breath and tried to make myself as small as possible. Ever so faintly, I could hear footsteps. Suddenly a man came into view right near my hiding spot. He was shuffling along on filthy sneakers. Everything he wore, from his grey overcoat to his black trousers appeared to be ragged and worn out. He moved remarkably quietly. He would take a step or two and then pause and listen. When he got to the corner at Church Street, he turned and looked down the long hallway. I was able to see the man's face. He had a full head of wild, dishevelled grey hair and a bushy grey beard. But what struck me the most was how old he seemed to be. He looked like he had to be at least eighty. And if I wasn't mistaken, the man seemed to be . . . frightened.

Is he as scared of me as I am of him? I wondered.

I stayed absolutely motionless as he moved past my hiding spot. The old man continued his pattern of moving a few steps and stopping to listen. He repeated this a few more times, then must have concluded that he had lost my trail, because he suddenly started walking purposefully toward the Wood Street end of the arena. He was surprisingly spry. My mind raced as I watched him.

I needed to make a decision and make it fast. My first instinct was to hightail it out of the Gardens and move on. After all, this guy could be dangerous. But I was not dumb enough to think there weren't dangerous people outside the building as well. Besides, the arena was relatively warm, it provided shelter, and it had a working washroom. Plus, something about this old guy fascinated me. Before I could tell myself it was a bad idea, I stepped out from my hiding spot and began to follow him silently down the concourse.

I was hiding in the darkened entrance of an archway on the uppermost concourse of the Gardens. I had spent over two hours stalking the man who appeared to be searching, very slowly and carefully, for me. I discovered that the easiest way to follow him undetected was if I mimicked his pattern of stopping to listen. If he turned down a hallway that ran off the main concourse, I would continue at the same pace. It took all my patience to hold back and trust that I would not lose the man's trail once he was out of my sight.

We continued our bizarre game of cat and mouse all over the arena. We went down narrow hallways, passed through entire sections of seats, climbed old abandoned escalators, and eventually worked our way over to the west side of the rink and up to the top concourse. I followed the man to an archway, where I stopped and watched as he climbed the steps to the uppermost row of seats in the arena. Then he shuffled along the back wall until he was at the approximate midpoint of the arena. A precarious-looking metal catwalk stretched out from the wall and connected to the long row of press boxes that appeared to be dangling from the roof of Maple Leaf Gardens.

A shiver ran down my spine as I stared, disbelieving, at the very catwalk that had haunted my nightmares ever since I was a little boy.

Surely he's not going to walk across that thing.

As if in answer to my thought, the man stepped up onto the catwalk, strode confidently across it, and disappeared into the press box.

A bead of sweat broke out on my forehead as I struggled to control my breathing. "Oh man, there's no way I'm going across that thing," I whispered to myself.

Since I didn't have any other plan, I decided to try and wait the man out. If I got bored, or hungry, I could always work my way down to the lower level and look for the storage room that I had used to enter the Gardens last night. I hoped that I'd be able to find it fairly easily in the daylight. I took off my backpack, leaned against the wall of the archway, and sat down. Then I began my stakeout.

———————————————

A metallic clanging caught my attention. I'd been dozing in the archway for the better part of an hour when I heard it, then saw the black silhouette working its way across the catwalk. I scrambled to my feet and dashed to the end of the archway. Zipping into the concourse, I flicked on my flashlight and saw another washroom. I ducked in. Then I turned off my light and willed my body to stay absolutely motionless.

A few seconds later, the silhouette of the mystery man emerged from the archway and went to the right.

I was just about to follow, when he turned around.

Uh-oh!

But he had just reached the top of the escalator and begun to descend it, oblivious to the fact that I was hiding only a short distance away.

Unlike earlier in the day, when he was looking for me, he now moved quickly. By the time I got down the escalator to the middle concourse, the man was gone. I peered down the hall toward Carlton Street.

Nothing.

I turned around just in time to see a bit of light disappearing along with the unmistakable sound of a closing door.

"Where are you off to, buddy?" I said under my breath.

I flicked my light back on and moved down the hallway in search of the door I'd heard closing. I found an old concession stand and carefully began to search it. I discovered a door at the back of the room. A skate lace was wrapped tightly around the handle, cleverly disabling the lock. I could see that the man had pulled the lace through the door jamb. He obviously used it to help pull open the door when he wanted to get back into the building.

Cautiously, I pushed on the door and immediately recognized the back alley that I had been in yesterday. I closed the door, taking extra care not to disturb the skate lace. Then I clambered down the fire escape and scurried over to the rusty iron gate. Following the old man's example, I removed the lock, stepped out onto Wood Street, then replaced the lock. I looked up and down the street and cursed. The mystery man had disappeared.

CHAPTER FOURTEEN

I sat by myself in the farthest corner of the food court and savoured my burger and fries. After I had lost the mystery man's trail, I decided to walk down to the Eaton Centre. I finally had to admit to myself that the guy scared me, and I needed to find another place to stay. But as soon as I got to the mall I realized I had made a mistake in coming here. The building was massive, and as I sat and watched the people stream by, I began to notice security guards . . . lots of them. My only chance to stay at the mall for the night would be to hide in a bathroom at closing time. That idea was both scary and gross. I drained my Coke and walked out onto Yonge Street.

As I made my way back to the Gardens, I thought about any other options that I had: I was certain that if I went to the police, they would make me go home. Not a chance. There were probably youth shelters in Toronto somewhere, but I had no idea how to find one, so that was out. In spite of the mystery man, hiding in the Gardens seemed to be my best—and only—option for now.

I stopped at a *Toronto Star* box and bought a newspaper. It was almost dark and I needed something to help me pass the evening hours alone. Slipping through the back gate behind the Gardens, I moved quietly through the alley, scaled the fire escape, and checked the skate lace. It hung dutifully in its place.

Where are you? I thought. *Well, if I hurry, at least I can get inside, and you might not know I'm here.*

I turned around and descended the fire escape. Without any trouble, I pried it open and squeezed through the storage room chute, dropping into the room much more confidently than I had the first time. My flashlight beam landed on the pile of old seats that had been crammed unceremoniously into a corner of the room. I pulled a red chair from the pile. Its frame was made of steel, but the seat and backrest were both padded.

Well, this'll be a lot better than sitting on the floor, I thought.

I put my backpack on and clenched my flashlight between my teeth. I picked up the chair—heavy, but I'd manage. After wrestling it into the hallway, I closed the door of the storage room, then hefted my new-found treasure and headed for the dim glow coming from Carlton Street.

I set up my chair near the box office in the main concourse, but before I had read a word, I put my newspaper down again. The entranceway where I sat was large and open, and I suddenly felt unprotected and exposed.

This is no good, I thought.

Heaving the red chair into my arms, I shuffled toward the large garbage pile that filled the corner where the Church Street hallway intersected with the Carlton Street concourse. I shoved the chair as far behind the pile as I could, then sat down and studied my shelter. Garbage bags, debris, and old construction materials made a high solid wall. It protected my back and stretched down to my left for about four or five metres. To my right was the paper-covered glass door that I had almost escaped through earlier in the day when I was hiding from the mystery man. This would be my emergency exit; I could bolt through it in a split second. The only vulnerability to my fortress was the entrance, which could be seen from the Church Street hallway. But if someone came along, I'd have time to escape through my side door.

Feeling pleased with myself and relatively safe, I turned my attention to my newspaper. At home I had never had downtime. I was always busy, always on the go, and it was strange to have so many hours to myself with little or nothing to do. I read the paper slowly, enjoying the comics and the sports section. I wished that I had a pen so that I could try the crossword puzzle.

And then an unfamiliar feeling came over me: I was bored. Fortunately, I was also tired. I tried to get comfortable in my chair. There was no way I was going to sleep on the floor again. The newspaper could double as a makeshift blanket, and I spread several sections out and covered myself. The loneliness that I had managed to keep at bay for most of the day began to creep back. I dozed off, promising myself that if things didn't improve tomorrow, I would have to come up with a different plan.

If anything, my second night in Maple Leaf Gardens was worse than the first. Last night, I had been so exhausted that I slept soundly. But try as I might, I just couldn't get comfortable in my red chair. I slept restlessly for an hour or two with my chin propped on my chest, but then I woke up to my neck muscles screaming in protest. Not only was my body not getting any rest, my mind wasn't either. I sat up and listened to the old building come alive with all kinds of sounds. The more it creaked and groaned, the more scared I got. When I was scared, the only thing I could think about was going home. My mind became a battlefield where my fear of being alone in the Gardens waged war against my anger toward my father. I spent a restless night dozing fitfully, waking frequently, and generally feeling lonely and miserable.

I had just dozed off as the first rays of morning light began to creep through the paper-covered windows—when a new sound woke me. I started to push myself up, but then froze, straining to detect any sound that was out of the ordinary for the building. At that moment, the mystery man flashed by the entrance to my hiding spot.

My mind raced with questions and emotions as I watched the man hustle down the Church Street corridor. I knew I should be scared of him. Okay, I admit it, I *was* scared of him, but I was also fascinated. "Who are you?" I hissed.

As the old guy disappeared around the corner at the end of the Church Street concourse, my curiosity got the best of me. Without thinking, I reached down and grabbed a large, odd-looking light bulb from amid the garbage, stood up, and heaved it as far as I could. It shattered on the floor with a tremendous racket. The man reappeared around the corner. As his eyes searched the room, he reminded me of the times when my class played blind man's bluff in drama class. It would have been funny, except the look on the old man's face made me feel sorry for him: he was genuinely scared. I sure knew that feeling.

The mystery man seemed to conclude that the light bulb had been thrown from the right, because he suddenly turned that way and disappeared through an archway.

"What? No, no, no. You're not going anywhere," I muttered.

I grabbed another light bulb and threw it. In the silence of the empty building, the smashing bulb sounded like a small explosion. I waited, holding my breath, and sure enough the old geezer peeked his head back into the main concourse.

"Who's there?" he asked in a ragged voice.

When he didn't get a response, the look on his face changed from fear to anger. "Why don't you go home?" he challenged.

What? I thought.

As if he was reading my mind, the old man shouted, "Yeah, you heard me. Why don't you go home? You should be home, watching TV, or out playing hockey. This is no place for a kid."

When he still couldn't find me, he let out a growl of frustration and turned his back. "Do what you want," he muttered. "But you can't stay here. This is *my* house."

At that moment, the seat of my red chair folded up with a loud, rusty-sounding groan. The man looked in my direction. I took a deep breath and moved out from behind my shelter. For a long time, the two of us just stared at each other. Then he moved toward me, his quizzical eyes never leaving my face. When he was about ten metres away, he stopped.

"What happened to your face?"

Without thinking, I reached up and touched my cheek. "Accident."

The man took another step and my hand shot out and grabbed the handle of my emergency exit door. He stopped. His eyes followed my movement and he nodded.

"That's right. Go on home," he said, waving his hands around at the old rink. "Like I said, this is no place for a kid."

My hand gripped the door handle, but I hesitated. "I can't go home," I said.

The old man nodded thoughtfully. "Because of your face?"

"Yeah, because of my face."

We continued to eye each other. I was trying to decide if I should run, and I was pretty sure he was willing me to run.

"What's your name?" I asked.

The question seemed to catch him by surprise. "My name? It's Scooter."

"Scooter, eh? My name's Jake."

"Jake," Scooter repeated. "Well, Jake, are you going to go home now, or what?"

Slowly I took my hand off the door handle. "No. I'm not going home."

Scooter blew out his breath. "I told you, you can't stay here."

"Come on, Scooter. It's a big rink. I promise I won't bother you."

Scooter turned and headed down the hallway. I stepped out from behind my hiding place and started after him.

"Look," I pleaded. "I'll stay one or two days and then I'll move on."

Scooter stopped walking and thrust his hands deep into the pockets of his jacket. "You can stay one night, but I want you gone in the morning."

I pumped my fist. "That's great, Scooter. Thanks a lot."

He began to walk away again.

"Hey, Scooter," I called.

He stopped and sighed. "What is it?"

"I was just wondering," I said. "I mean, are you hungry?"

Scooter turned around and smiled sadly at me. "Kid," he answered, "I'm always hungry."

We walked along Yonge until we reached Tim Hortons. I grabbed the handle and gave the door a shove.

Scooter stamped his feet against the cold. "I can't go in there, Jake."

I was confused. "Why not?"

Scooter raised an are-you-serious eyebrow. "Because I don't have any money."

I groaned at my own stupidity. "Oh man, I'm sorry."

"That's okay, forget it."

"I'll tell you what. Let's go in and I'll buy—my treat."

I tried to ignore the stares as we stood in line to order. We must have made quite a pair, the kid with the busted-up face and the old, homeless man. Scooter seemed to be having trouble seeing the menu, so I read it to him. He settled on a bowl of chili and a cup of coffee, and his face lit up when the lady asked him what kind of doughnut he wanted to go with his combo. He pointed to an old-fashioned glazed.

"Good call," I said.

"It looks really good."

I smiled. "It sure does."

I put on a brave face and tried not to show my distress at suddenly doubling the amount that I had expected to pay. But when I saw how Scooter savoured every bite of that doughnut, I decided that it had been worth it.

While he was sipping his coffee, Scooter said, "I knew him, you know."

I looked up from my soup. "Knew who?"

"Tim Horton."

"Oh yeah?" I went back to my soup. I didn't have a lot of experience with old people, but I figured that they were as likely to make up a story as anyone else.

"He was a hell of a defenceman. Tough as nails." Scooter took another sip of his coffee and said nothing more.

When we had finished our meal, we walked back to the Gardens. Scooter told me that the secret to surviving life on the streets in winter was to stay warm.

"Only go outside when you have to," he said.

When we were back inside, Scooter thanked me again for lunch. "Tonight I'll take you out for dinner, and this time it'll be my treat."

I wasn't sure how Scooter could take me out for dinner if he didn't have any money, but I agreed.

"I'll see you later," he said, leaving me in the main concourse.

"Where are you going?"

"To have a nap," he called back over his shoulder. "I'll meet you here later."

I wanted to chase after him or find an excuse to keep him

around, but Scooter had already vanished and I was alone again. Miserable, I sank back into my red chair. I tried rereading the newspaper, but I was soon bored again. The Gardens seemed to be laughing at me with its symphony of creaks and groans.

"Shut up," I muttered.

I needed something to occupy my time. I stood up and looked around. Time to do some more exploring.

I had walked for kilometres around the old arena; up escalators and down back hallways. I found the Leafs' dressing room and Harold Ballard's famous bunker, the room at the end of the arena that the former owner of the Leafs used to sit in when he watched his team play. My feet were sore and I was tired. I was quickly learning that one of the hardest things about life on the streets was occupying your mind. I was sitting in my red chair with my feet up, reading my newspaper, when Scooter emerged from the darkness.

"Sorry, Jake, did I scare you?"

"Just a little."

"Let's get some dinner," he said gruffly.

This time it was Scooter's turn to be the tour guide. We trudged along Yonge Street for a long time, finally stopping in front of a building. Scooter opened the door.

"What's this?" I asked.

"Dinner," Scooter replied. "My treat."

The sign over the door read Christian Charity Soup Kitchen. I didn't know what to do. I didn't want to look like a snob, but I'd had no idea we were going to a soup kitchen. The nondescript room was filled with row upon row of neatly organized folding tables and chairs. At the back of the room a man stood behind a table, serving up meals to a long line of people, each waiting silently for a turn. I had never seen so many homeless people in my life. They were young and old, male and female, black, brown, and white.

As we shuffled closer to the man behind the table, I could hear him speaking kindly to each person. He called most of them by name. When Scooter got to the front of the line, the man smiled at him.

"Good evening, Scooter. How are you tonight?"

"Evening, Reverend Pete. I'm fine, thank you."

Reverend Pete looked at me and raised his eyebrows ever so slightly. "Who's your friend, Scooter?"

"This here is Jake."

"Welcome, Jake," the Reverend said.

"Thank you, sir," I answered.

Reverend Pete handed me a plate that smelled better than it looked. "Enjoy your meal."

I nodded politely and followed Scooter to a table. I tried a bite and was relieved to find that, like the smell, the taste was better than the appearance. In fact, it was quite delicious. While we ate, I asked Scooter if he knew any other people at the soup kitchen. Scooter didn't know much about them.

"Well, where do they all live?" I asked.

"Same place as me," he answered.

I was shocked. "You mean all these people are living at the Gardens?"

Scooter laughed quietly. "No, no. They're like me. They've found someplace warm."

"How do you know?" I asked.

Scooter shrugged. "Because if they weren't warm, they'd be dead."

I was wiping up the last drops of my dinner with a piece of bread when Reverend Pete came over to our table.

"Mind if I join you?" he asked.

"Not at all, Reverend," Scooter replied.

The Reverend sat down beside me. "Are you okay, son?" he asked.

"Yes, sir," I said. "Dinner was delicious."

Reverend Pete chuckled softly. "No, Jake, not your meal. I meant are *you* okay?"

I looked at Scooter and the old man said, "It's okay, Jake. You can trust the Reverend."

"I'm okay," I mumbled, looking down at my plate.

"Is there anyone you'd like me to call?" Reverend Pete asked. "Can I give you a ride somewhere?"

I shook my head.

"Jake," Reverend Pete said gently.

I looked up.

"Would you like to tell me who hurt you?"

Again, I shook my head.

"Son, it's my duty under the law to report to the police if I have reason to believe that a child is in danger. And judging by your face, I'd say it's safe to say that you are."

At the mention of the police, I leapt to my feet.

Pete held up his hands. "Easy, kiddo. Just take it easy."

"N-no police," I stammered. I looked around the room,

located the front door, and was considering making a run for it, when Pete stood up.

"Just take it easy," he repeated. "Do you have a place to stay tonight?"

I nodded. "Yes, Scooter says I can stay with him as long as I promise to stay out of his way."

Reverend Pete looked from me to Scooter. "He'll be safe, Scooter? And warm?"

Scooter shrugged. "Warm enough."

Reverend Pete turned his attention back to me. "I'll tell you honestly, son, I do not like this idea. Are you sure there isn't anyone I can call?"

When I shook my head again, he said, "Wait here a second, I have something for you."

He disappeared into a backroom and I had a sickening feeling that he had snuck off to call the police, but a few moments later, the large man returned with something tucked under his arm. A sleeping bag! He handed it to me and I accepted it gratefully.

"If you change your mind, Jake, just come and see me tomorrow and I'll take you anywhere you want to go: home, the police, you name it."

I clutched the sleeping bag like it was a life ring. "Thank you, Reverend."

That night, I sat in the main lobby of Maple Leaf Gardens, bundled up in my new sleeping bag and reading the *Toronto Star* by the glow of the Carlton Street lights. On the way home from the soup kitchen I had stopped in front of the newspaper box and tried to decide if I should part with a precious loonie. Scooter asked me what I was doing.

"I want a newspaper, but I don't want to spend the money."

Scooter nodded and walked over to the machine. He started jimmying the handle while repeatedly pushing the coin return button. Then he gently tapped the side of the box. The door popped open like magic and Scooter reached in and grabbed a newspaper.

"There ya go, Jake. One *Toronto Star*."

I laughed as Scooter shuffled off. "Thanks a lot, Scooter."

Scooter had left me in the lobby a while ago, and I was just about ready to turn in for the night when I heard him coming down the corridor. He was dragging something along behind him. He set the object down beside me. It was a piece of foam padding.

"Jake, I wanted to thank you again for buying me lunch today."

"That's okay," I replied.

Scooter shook his head. "No, you don't understand. What you did today was not okay, it was . . ." He paused, looking for the right words. "It was unusual. I've been living on the streets a long time, and ain't nobody ever bought me a meal. Anyway, good night, Jake."

"Good night, Scooter," I said to the darkness into which he'd already disappeared.

I got up from my red chair and arranged my sleeping bag on top of the foam. Then I hunkered down inside it and sighed contentedly.

"Perfect," I whispered. I was asleep in no time.

CHAPTER FIFTEEN

The next few days passed uneventfully. My biggest enemies continued to be loneliness, boredom, and fear. I didn't have a TV, a computer, or music, and even though I was in the largest city in Canada, I really had nowhere to go. I tried to combat the loneliness and boredom by spending as much time as I could with Scooter. He seemed to have forgotten about his threat to kick me out of the Gardens. In fact, I think he enjoyed having my company as much as I was beginning to enjoy his. It was at night that I really struggled. The foam pad and the sleeping bag provided some warmth and comfort, but they couldn't hide the fact that I was sleeping in an abandoned building, and this was when I would get scared. Physical exhaustion was also an ally because if I was tired enough, I would fall asleep before homesickness and fear took over for the night.

Something else was bothering me too. I was really starting

to worry about my mom. I tried to fall asleep quickly each night before I had time to feel guilty about leaving her behind in the house with Dad.

Reverend Pete's soup kitchen served lunch and dinner, so twice a day we would leave the warmth of the Gardens and head over there. As a special treat, I would stop at Tim Hortons and buy Scooter an old-fashioned glazed. He never asked me why I didn't buy one for myself and I didn't want to tell him that I was almost out of money. As thanks for the doughnut, Scooter would jimmy the *Toronto Star* box to get me a newspaper. Then we would sit in the front row of the arena in what used to be the best seats in the house and I would read it out loud. Scooter's favourite section was the sports. He was particularly interested in how the Leafs were doing.

The night before, the Leafs had been trounced by the Chicago Black Hawks. The articles on the Leafs' latest loss spanned three full pages. When I was finished reading, Scooter regaled me with stories about the Black Hawks.

"When I was younger, I used to get sticks that the players had used. Usually they were broken, but sometimes I'd get one that wasn't."

"Oh yeah?" I said. "What did you do with them?"

"I sold them to people outside the arena. One night Bobby Hull signed a stick for me. I made a lot of money that night."

I was intrigued. "I'd love to get a signed stick from *Brett* Hull."

"Who's Brett Hull?"

I laughed. "Are you kidding? He's one of the best goal scorers in the history of the league. He's in the Hall of Fame."

Scooter nodded. "Yeah, that's him. Pure goal scorer, cannon of a shot, Hall of Fame, but his name's Bobby, not Brett."

I smiled at my friend. "Okay, Scooter, take it easy."

"Did you know that the last game ever played here was between the Leafs and the Black Hawks?" Scooter asked.

"No."

"It was a good one," he added.

"Did you watch it on TV?" I asked.

"Nope."

"You were *here* for the last game?"

"Sat right over there," he said, pointing to a section of seats that looked like they'd been right behind the Leafs bench. "When the game ended, the crowd seemed to want to hold onto the building as long as possible," Scooter recalled. "People gathered out on Carlton Street and had a giant party. When everyone finally left, and they locked up the building, I stayed behind. I've been here ever since."

My jaw dropped. "Do you mean to tell me that you've been living in the Gardens since it *closed*?"

"February 13, 1999."

I wanted to ask how Scooter had gone from watching the game from the best seats in the house to, well, just sitting in the empty house, but before I could figure out a way to ask him, he continued with his story.

"For the most part, the building has sat empty. They left the water on and the toilets working because every now and then they film something here. They did a movie about boxing once. But, basically, I've had the place to myself."

"What do you do when there are people here?"

Scooter looked up at the old press box. "Stay out of the way," he said. "For the most part it's been okay. The only thing that bothered me was when they ripped the seats and the boards out." He looked around sadly at his "home." The old girl's never been the same since."

I followed Scooter's gaze. I was never inside the arena in its heyday, but I couldn't help but share in his sadness.

The next day dawned clear and crisp. I lay awake for the longest time and stayed tucked in my sleeping bag. It was too cold to get up. Besides, there wasn't much else to do until Scooter came down from his hiding spot in the press box. Today was December 24, Christmas Eve.

I was so homesick. No, *homesick* wasn't the right word. I was "Mom sick." Every day I missed her more, and my guilt about leaving her alone with my dad got worse. When would I ever see her again? I rolled over and sighed. As long as Dad was around, I didn't really see how it could happen.

Discouraged, I got up and went to the washroom. Of all the places in the Gardens, the washroom was the spot that scared me the most. It was so dark and creepy and I was terrified that my flashlight batteries would die while I was in there. Quickly, I washed my face and brushed my teeth with the new toothbrush Reverend Pete had given me. I could put up with not showering, but I couldn't stand the feel of the crusties that built up in my mouth when my teeth weren't brushed. I looked into the cracked mirror and tried to smile at my reflection.

"It's okay, buddy. You'll see Mom again."

I tried to convince myself that I actually believed that.

Reverend Pete was wearing a Christmas hat with *Santa's Little Helper* embroidered across the fake white, fur-trimmed edge. I smiled as I accepted a grilled cheese sandwich from him. This man was a lot of things—kind, compassionate, thoughtful. But *little* certainly wasn't a word that I would use to describe him.

As usual, the Reverend joined Scooter and me after he had served the last person. He lowered himself into a folding chair, which groaned under his weight. "How are you today, Scooter?"

Scooter grumbled a "Fine, thanks" as he chewed his sandwich.

"And how are you on this cold Christmas Eve, Jake?"

"Okay, Reverend," I replied.

"Your eye is healing up nicely," he noted. "So, Jake, is there anything I can do for you today?" He had asked me the same question every day since we'd met.

And every day I answered with "No, thank you."

Pete sighed and looked down at his hands. "Son," he began, "may I make an observation?"

"Sure."

"Okay, here's how I see things. You are well dressed, you appear to be drug free, and you seem to be an intelligent kid." He looked up at me. "How am I doing so far?"

I smiled cautiously, not sure where he was going with this. "Pretty good."

"You've also been beaten up, perhaps on more than one occasion."

I started making designs on my paper plate by dragging my pickle through my ketchup.

"Jake, I'll bet you one grilled cheese sandwich that the reason you ran away is that someone at home is hurting you."

I continued to swirl a figure eight through my ketchup.

"Jake," Reverend Pete said.

I looked up slowly.

"Am I right or wrong?"

Tears welled up in my eyes and threatened to spill over. "You're not wrong," I said.

"Who is it?" he asked. "Is it your father?"

The dam that I was trying to hold back suddenly burst and a cascade of tears coursed down my cheeks.

Reverend Pete seemed to be taken aback by the crying. Suddenly he got to his feet and left the table.

I wiped my eyes with the back of my hand.

"I'm sorry, Jake," Scooter said.

"Not your fault."

"No," Scooter continued, "I mean I wish that there was something that I could do to help."

I was about to tell Scooter that he had done more to help me than he could ever possibly know, but we were interrupted by the return of Reverend Pete. He plunked a new plate of food down in front of me.

"There you go, Jake. One grilled cheese sandwich. Extra pickles."

I smiled at him. "But you won the bet—shouldn't you get the sandwich?"

He shrugged.

As I tore into it, he said, "The offer still stands. If there is anything I can do for you, let me know. And, Jake, let me know sooner than later. If you can't go home, you do have other options. I could take you to a youth shelter, for example. But trust me, son, the street is no place for a kid."

Pete left me to my sandwich.

I looked over at Scooter.

"See? I told ya." Scooter grinned. Then he reached over and stole all of my extra pickles.

Snow fell gently as we walked up Yonge Street amid a throng. Scooter tried not to look over at Tim Hortons, like a little kid trying to be on his best behaviour. Subtly, I reached into my pocket and pulled out the last of my money.

$1.27.

There really wasn't much you could buy with $1.27. But I could get my friend a doughnut on Christmas Eve.

"Can I get you an old-fashioned glazed?" I asked.

"If it's not too much trouble." Scooter practically ran toward the restaurant. I had to hustle to keep up.

When he was finished his doughnut, we headed back to the Gardens. Scooter stopped at the newspaper box and worked his magic on it. He was reaching in to grab a paper when he froze.

By then I had figured out that Scooter probably couldn't read, yet he was studying the cover of the paper.

"What's so interesting?" I asked.

Scooter handed me the newspaper. "It's not every day that I

know the person on the front page."

I gasped. There, staring back at me, was my own picture. It was this year's school photo. Now it took up most of the front page of the *Toronto Star*, smack dab under the large headline:

STILL NO SIGN OF MISSING BOY

"I guess that we have some reading to do," Scooter said.

CHAPTER SIXTEEN

STILL NO SIGN OF MISSING BOY
By Garrett Mercer

Rebecca Dumont sits in the front room of her North York home and gazes out the window. She's been doing a lot of that since her twelve-year-old son, Jake, disappeared ten days ago.

"I have no idea where he could be," says Dumont. "I'm just hoping that if Jake sees this article he'll know that his mom loves him very much and hopes he's safe."

Police are not offering many details, although they have indicated there is strong evidence the missing boy ran away. At the time of his disappearance, he was a star GTHL Major Peewee player, leading the division in scoring, according to Alistair Caldwell, league spokesman. Caldwell said he was unable to offer further comment.

Betsy O'Toole, the principal at Terry Fox Elementary, told the Star *that Jake Dumont has been enrolled in that school since kindergarten, and that he is a model student, his grades "above average."*

Continued on page A16.

I flipped to the back of the newspaper and finished reading the article. Then I turned back to the front page and stared at my picture before rereading the article.

"Well, Jake," Scooter said. "I can see that you have a lot to think about. I guess I'll go and grab a nap."

"I can read you the rest of the newspaper," I said. "I don't mind."

"Don't worry about it, kid. I'll see you later for dinner."

After Scooter left, I tried to take my mind off things with the sports section, but that didn't work. I read the article through for a third time—and then it hit me. Dad wasn't quoted anywhere.

That's weird, I thought. *Dad always does the talking.*

What if he didn't say anything because he didn't want me to come home? Angrily, I threw the newspaper on the ground. I was so frustrated and confused. I really wanted to talk to my mom. I wanted to go home.

"I can't believe I'm living in this rat hole," I muttered. I looked around the Gardens and sighed. I had absolutely no idea what I should do.

The soup kitchen was decorated with strings of coloured lights, and the folding tables were covered with red and green paper tablecloths, but most of the people there didn't seem to want to be reminded about Christmas.

Scooter and I ate our meal in silence. I was still thinking about the newspaper article, and Scooter was focused on his mashed potatoes and stuffing.

When Reverend Pete sat down with us there was no small talk or his usual offer to help. Instead, he placed a copy of the *Toronto Star* in front of me.

"Have you seen this?"

I put down my fork. "Yeah. Scooter and I read it earlier."

"Your mother is worried about you," Reverend Pete said.

I slammed my hand on the table. "Do you think I don't know that?" I snapped. "I'm worried about her too. I should never have left her behind with my dad."

"It's okay," the Reverend said calmly. "But I think it's time that you accepted some help."

I could feel the tears coming to my eyes again. "I wanna go home," I snuffled.

Reverend Pete nodded. "We can get you home. Just let me help. I can drive you there right now."

"But, Reverend Pete, it's Christmas Eve. What about your family?"

Pete spread out his arms and looked around the soup kitchen. "This is my family," he said. "It's no problem. I'll drive you."

When the last person had left, Reverend Pete locked the front door and led Scooter and me into the back room. It was a large, efficient-looking kitchen. Several people were still bustling about, washing dishes and drying pots and pans.

Pete spoke to the lady who appeared to be in charge. "Can you close up, please, Catherine? I have an errand to run."

Catherine plunged her hands into the dishwater and smiled. "No problem, Reverend. Merry Christmas."

We stepped out into a small alley. There, wedged into an impossibly small parking space, was a rusty, old Honda Civic.

While it was warming up, Pete chuckled softly. He twisted around toward Scooter and said, "I just realized, Scooter, that I don't know where you live."

Scooter hesitated. I knew that he had never told anyone where he lived. Finally, he answered, "I live at Maple Leaf Gardens."

Pete laughed "How on earth . . . ? Wait, I don't even want to know," he said. "Well then, I certainly don't need any directions. Shall I drop you off at the front door or the back?"

Scooter laughed too. "The back door would be just fine, thank you."

When we pulled onto Wood Street, Scooter directed Reverend Pete to the back corner by the old iron gate. He parked the car, and within a few minutes, Scooter and I were in and out of the arena, carrying all of my belongings.

Pete opened the hatchback so I could pile in my stuff.

Scooter was standing with his hands jammed deep into his pockets. An idea came to me. "Scooter, why don't you come home with me?"

Scooter didn't answer right away. Finally, he shook his head. "This is my home, Jake."

"It's Christmas. You shouldn't be by yourself."

Scooter shrugged. "Jake, to you it's Christmas, but to me it's Wednesday."

I tried to argue, but my voice caught in my throat and I felt like I was going to start crying again. I didn't know what to do.

"I'm sorry to waste your time," I said to Reverend Pete, "but I can't leave Scooter here by himself."

"Oh no, Jake," he protested. "You need to go home."

I shook my head. "But Scooter's all alone."

The Reverend looked like he was trying not to get angry. "Son," he said, keeping his voice calm. "This is an abandoned building. It's not safe—"

"Safe enough for Scooter," I interrupted.

"Jake," Scooter said quietly. Reverend Pete and I both turned to look at him. "It's time for you to go home, my friend."

"But—"

He held up his hand to cut me off. "The Reverend's right. You go on now. Go home and see your mom."

I didn't know what to do. I looked at my friend for a long time. He waited patiently for me to reach my decision. Finally, I walked over and gave him a hug.

"Merry Christmas," I whispered.

Then I turned and got into the car.

CHAPTER SEVENTEEN

Reverend Pete navigated the streets of North York, doing his best to follow my directions. As we drove, we discussed the *Toronto Star* article, and I told Reverend Pete my theory that my dad didn't want me to come home because he hadn't even bothered talking to the paper.

"Maybe he's not even there," the Reverend said. "Is there any chance your mother made him leave?"

"I don't know. I kind of doubt it."

We pulled onto my street and I showed him which one of the identical bungalows was mine. Pete nodded, but drove past it until he was around a corner and parked out of sight of the house.

"Jake, I want you to stay in the car for a few minutes," he said.

"Why?" I asked. I already had my hand on the door handle.

"Let me go and ring the bell. If your father is home, I'll just say that I have the wrong house."

"Then what?"

"Then we go to the police. I'd feel better about them making the decision to take you home. And I think your father would be less likely to hurt you if the police were involved. If he's not home, we'll sit down with your mother and figure some things out."

I opened the door. "I want to come with you."

"Wait!" Pete commanded. He heaved himself out of the car. "At least stay out of sight while I do the talking," he pleaded.

"Okay," I agreed. "Wait here for a second."

I cut across my neighbour's lawn and sprinted toward the corner of our house. When I got there, I waved at the Reverend. I watched him bustle up the front walk. Just before he rang the bell he gave me a quick glance. He looked nervous.

Ready? he mouthed.

I nodded and he rang the bell.

I heard someone moving around inside the house and then the porch light snapped on over Pete's head.

The door opened. "May I help you?" Mom asked.

"I'm sorry to bother you, ma'am. My name is Reverend Peter Ambrose and I'm from the Christian Charity Church in Toronto."

Apparently, his introduction meant nothing to Mom. Pete cleared his throat and tried again. "Ma'am, I was wondering if I could speak to your husband."

"Why?" Mom asked suspiciously.

Reverend Pete said, "I'm sorry, I can't tell you that. But it's very important that I speak to him."

"He's not here right now. If you don't mind . . ." I could hear the door closing.

"Rebecca, wait!" Pete exclaimed.

Oh no, I thought.

Mom must have been thinking the same thing. "How do you know my name?" She sounded scared. "I think you'd better leave."

"Please," Pete pleaded, "I know that I'm a complete stranger, and this must seem a bit bizarre, but this relates to your son, Jake."

I could hear Mom gasp. "What do you know about Jake?" she demanded.

Pete held his ground. "Is your husband home?"

"No!" I could hear the panic in her voice.

"Will he be home tonight?"

"No! Now tell me what you know about my son, or I'm calling the police."

Pete held up his hands and smiled. "Rebecca, I have a very special present for you." He motioned me with his hand. Then he turned back to Mom and said, "Merry Christmas, Rebecca."

I stepped out from behind the corner of the house.

"Jake!" Mom yelled. She flung her arms around me and held me in the tightest hug that I had ever felt. I hugged back just as fiercely. She plastered my face with kisses and then squeezed me again. "My baby, are you okay?"

"I'm fine," I answered.

Our reunion was interrupted by a loud honking sound. Reverend Pete was blowing his nose and weeping openly. "Merry Christmas, Jake," he sobbed.

I laughed. "Thanks, Reverend. Mom, this is Reverend Pete."

"Pleased to meet you," she said. "And thank you. This is the best Christmas present in the world."

Reverend Pete grinned and blew his nose again.

"Okay, you two, come on inside and warm up. I'll put the coffee on. Jake, you must have quite a story to tell."

I turned to Reverend Pete. "Will you please come in?"

Pete looked really sad.

"Jake, I can't leave you here. You're not safe." He looked at Mom. "You're not safe either. I just brought Jake home so that you'd know he was okay. Now he needs to grab a few things quickly, maybe a change of clothes, and we need to move fast, in case your husband comes home."

Mom held up her hands. "Reverend—"

Pete cut her off. "Look, Rebecca. I'm sorry but I can't leave Jake here. Come with us and I'll take you to a shelter. Or say good night to him. Your choice."

Mom placed one hand on the Reverend's arm and the other on his shoulder. "Reverend Ambrose, a few minutes ago you asked me to trust you. Now I'm asking you to do the same thing. Trust me. We have time for a cup of coffee."

She turned and headed into the house. "Hurry up, you two. You're letting all the heat out."

Pete and I looked at each other, and then we followed her inside.

CHAPTER EIGHTEEN

By the time I swallowed the last few drops of my hot chocolate, I had recounted most of my story from the past ten days. Mom did her best not to interrupt, but she gasped and covered her mouth when I talked about sleeping in the subway station and breaking into Maple Leaf Gardens. Although she tried to hide it, I could tell that she was horrified by the fact that I had spent so much time with a homeless person.

Reverend Pete seemed to sense it too. "With all due respect, Mrs. Dumont, you should know that Scooter is a kind and gentle person."

Mom blushed slightly. "I'm sorry, Reverend. It's just that . . ." She looked for the right way to voice her feelings, then seemed to think better of it and changed the subject. "I'm just glad you're safe, Jake."

Now it was my turn to ask questions, and I decided to start with the most important one.

"Where's Dad?"

Mom put down her mug.

"You know," she said, more to Reverend Pete than to me, "I never had the courage to stand up to my husband when he was hurting Jake, and because I did nothing, Jake ran away." She looked at me and continued. "When I realized that you were gone, something inside me snapped. Your dad had succeeded in driving away the only person that I have ever truly loved."

Mom looked down at her coffee cup and laughed softly, but without humour.

"What's funny about that?" I asked.

"It's just that, Jake, you were probably safer in an abandoned building with a homeless man than you were living in your own home."

"Mom, it's not your fault—"

"I should have protected you," she said. "Anyway, when I found the note that you left in your room, I confronted him about it. Do you know what he did?"

I shook my head.

"He *denied* it." I had never heard her speak with so much anger. "He *denied* it," she repeated. "Then he stormed out of the house and jumped into the van and said he was going to look for you. I called the police, and by the time your dad came home there were two officers here."

She paused and took a sip of her coffee. "There were two officers, one male and one female. The male officer went with your father to look in your room for clues. The female officer stayed with me. I showed her your note."

"What did she do?" I asked.

"She asked me if I needed protection. I said that I did. When your father came back with the other officer, she said, 'Sir, I need you to collect some personal belongings, and then I need you to leave the house.'"

"Whoa!" I exclaimed. "And then what happened?"

Mom smiled sadly at the memory.

"They told him he could go quietly or they could force him out and get a restraining order. Fortunately, he didn't put up a fight, and he's now staying across town with a friend from work. The female officer, Constable Rodriquez, gave me her business card and wrote down the name of a lawyer who specializes in domestic abuse. I phoned him, and by the end of the day, I had new locks on the doors and that was that."

"Incredible," I said, as I tried to take in all this new information. "You were amazingly brave, Mom."

Mom smiled sadly. "Not as brave as you, Jake."

"Well, I think you are both very brave," Reverend Pete said.

I had been so absorbed in Mom's story that I had almost forgotten he was still there.

Reverend Pete got up from the table. "I really needed to know that you two are safe. And now that I know, I should probably be going."

Mom and I both protested and told him that he was welcome to stay, but he brushed us off. He zipped up his coat and held out his hand to Mom.

"Good luck to you," he said. Then he handed her a business card and told her to have the police contact him if they had any questions.

"Thank you for bringing Jake home," she said. "Now if you'll excuse me, I'd better go and call the police and let them know he's safe."

I walked Reverend Pete to the door, and he bundled me into a massive bear hug. "Look after your mother. And look after yourself, too," he said.

I smiled up at the big man. "I will. And, Reverend?"

"Yes, Jake?"

"Take good care of Scooter."

"That's a promise," he called over his shoulder as he started down the walkway. "Merry Christmas!"

I stared at my clock radio and watched it turn from 11:59 p.m. to 12 a.m. I had been tossing and turning for an hour, but I couldn't get comfortable. I wasn't overly excited about Christmas. When you've been living on the streets, presents, ribbons, and bows fall a long way down your list of priorities. I had so much on my mind. I was worried about Scooter. I worried I wouldn't be allowed to play with my team again. I worried about my dad, where he was, and what he was doing. Generally . . . I just worried. As the clock ticked toward 1 a.m., I pulled my duvet off the bed, grabbed my pillow, and curled up on the floor. The carpet was just about the same firmness as my mat had been at Maple Leaf Gardens. I snuggled under the duvet, muttered "Merry Christmas" to myself, and fell asleep.

Christmas morning arrived with very little fanfare. I was just glad to be home and Mom was just happy to have me home. In the afternoon, we curled up on the couch together and watched Jimmy Stewart in *It's a Wonderful Life*. Mom emailed Coach

Madigan to let him know I was safe, but she wouldn't let me call him until Boxing Day.

"Let the man have one day where he doesn't have to think about hockey," she said.

We went to a restaurant for Christmas dinner. When I was missing, the last thing Mom could think about was buying a turkey. I didn't mind. The steak that the restaurant served was tastier than Mom's turkey anyway.

At exactly 9 a.m. on Boxing Day, the earliest Mom would let me phone, I dialled Coach Madigan's number. A sleepy voice answered the phone.

"Hello?"

"Coach Madigan?"

"Yes?"

"It's Jake."

The sleep vanished from Madigan's voice. "Jake!" he exclaimed. "How are you?"

"I'm okay. I got home late on Christmas Eve."

"I'm so glad you're safe."

"Coach?"

"Yes?"

"Am I still eligible to play?"

"What do you mean?" he asked.

"Well, I've been away for a while, missed some games," I said. "Am I still allowed to play?"

"Of course you are, Jake. You're part of our team, always have been. The boys know that you've gone through a tough time, and they'll be excited to have you back."

I felt like a huge weight had just been lifted off my shoulders. "Thanks, Coach."

I could feel Coach smiling at his end of the phone. "We have practice tomorrow. I'll see you then. Oh, and Jake?"

"Yes?"

"I'm so glad you're home, buddy."

"Thanks."

That afternoon, Constable Rodriquez, the police officer who helped Mom, came over and interviewed me. It was hard explaining my story to her, and I thought she was going to lecture me about running away, but she was really nice and a good listener. When I was done, she gave me her business card.

"If you ever feel like you need to run away again, I want you to call me first, okay? I'll do everything I can to help you."

I put her card in my pocket. "I think I can do that," I said.

The rink had always been a place where I felt like I belonged. But on my first day back, I wasn't so sure. I had never been as nervous as I was right now. I picked up my hockey stick and tore off the tape. Maybe a new tape job would make me feel better. As I rummaged through my bag, looking for a roll, the dressing room door opened. I had just enough time to look up before being hammered by a flying tackle hug from Freddie.

"Jake!" He beamed. "Are you okay? Where have you been? What were you thinking? Are you out of your mind?"

Freddie fired questions at me, until he eventually calmed down enough to allow me to talk. By the time the rest of the team began to filter in, we had pretty well caught up with each other's lives.

On the ice, I felt stiff and sore. I was surprised at how little energy I had and how bad my stick handling was. Toward the end of practice, Coach Madigan called for a scrimmage. I was reunited with Joey and Lyle. We were being hemmed in our own end and we couldn't get anything going. I fought for the puck behind my own net. I made a quick stick check and stole the puck and bolted out, firing a pass up the right boards to Joey. He chipped the puck out off the boards, past the defenceman. I picked up the puck just outside the blue line and took off at full speed. After I fed a cross-ice pass over to Lyle, he took the puck wide on the other defenceman and broke for the net. At the last second he slid the puck back across to me, and I hammered it past Freddie and into the top corner.

Madigan blew his whistle. "All right, that's it, boys. Good practice. Jake!"

I skated over to him.

Coach smiled and whacked me on the shin pads with his stick. "It's good to have you back."

On the morning of January fifth, I trudged through a gentle snowfall on my way back to school. I was shivering, but it was more from nerves than from the cold as I reached the area where the grade sevens usually hung out. A cluster of boys were huddled together trying to stay warm. I stood quietly off to the side, not sure what I should do next. Then one of them noticed me. "Hey, man, you're back!"

Stilts turned around. "Jake!" he exclaimed.

He grabbed and hugged me. He didn't seem to notice the looks of disgust that our classmates were exchanging.

"Hi, Stilts," I said when I was finally freed from his grasp.

When the bell rang, I think I was the only kid standing in that line who was excited about being back at school. It was way better than sitting in an abandoned building, day after day, with nothing to do. As we shuffled through the doors, Mr. Hamilton greeted each student.

"Hi, Mr. Hamilton," I said.

"Jake!" he exclaimed and grabbed me in my second hug of the last five minutes. "We were so glad to hear you made it home safe and sound. Welcome back."

"I'll catch up on the work I missed," I promised.

Hamilton dismissed this with a wave of his hand. "That's not important, Jake. All that matters is that you're safe."

I was still reeling from the shock of a teacher saying not to worry about schoolwork as I took my seat. Sam was already at her desk, copying out the day's word problem. I was suddenly nervous again.

I hope she's as excited to see me as I am to see her, I thought as I sat down beside her.

"Hi, Sam."

Sam continued working on the word problem.

I guessed she didn't hear me.

"Hi, Sam," I said a little more loudly.

Again, she ignored me. I felt like I'd been kicked in the stomach. I thought she was my friend! I thought she liked me! Confused and hurt, I tried to concentrate on the word problem.

Sam maintained the cold shoulder routine for the first hour of the day. Around ten o'clock, I tried again.

"Sam, can I borrow your calculator?" I asked.

"Math is over," she grunted.

"Can I borrow a pencil?"

"You're supposed to be reading," she snapped.

"Can I borrow a book?"

Sam slammed her novel down on the top of her desk and hissed, "What is your problem?"

I grinned. "My problem is that I don't have a book."

Sam picked up her novel. "Try your desk, moron."

My grin vanished as I reached into my desk and pulled out my novel. I tried to read, but it was a lost cause. There was no way I could concentrate.

At the end of the day, I grabbed my things and headed out the door. I was walking up the street in front of our school when my name was called. I looked around and there was Sam, hustling to catch up.

Now what? I just kept walking.

"Jake! Jake, please!"

I didn't stop.

She caught up to me and grabbed my arm. Her face was flushed from the cold and from the exertion of trying to chase me.

"What do you want?" I asked a little more harshly than I had meant to.

"I . . ." she started. "I'm sorry for the way I acted today."

"Oh." I wasn't expecting that. "You sure were mad at me."

"I know. I don't know why I was so angry. It's just that . . ." She paused, looking for the right words. "I dunno. I was so scared and upset when you ran away. I worried about you for a long time. And then when I saw you today, it just made me more mad than glad, I guess. Does that make any sense?"

I smiled. "Yeah, it makes sense."

Sam readjusted her backpack with her right hand. She held out her left hand and asked, "Are we okay, then?"

I felt silly shaking her hand, but I did anyway. "Yeah, we're good."

Then, for some reason, I didn't let go of her hand. Sam didn't seem interested in letting go either, so we held hands as we walked up the street. I was surprised to realize that holding hands with Sam generated far more warmth than all the hugs that I had received from everyone I'd ever hugged put together.

Cool, I thought to myself, as I grinned nervously.

CHAPTER NINETEEN

On the second day back at school, I was hit with that annual bombshell that most kids dread—speeches. Maybe keeners and the self-confident kids enjoy them, but most of us, especially quiet kids like me, view public speaking right up there with a trip to the dentist. The idea of standing at the front of the room with the whole class watching terrified me.

Mr. Hamilton told us, "You guys need to start challenging yourselves a bit. I believe I speak for all of us when I say that no one cares about your goldfish or your hamster." A few of the kids laughed. Hamilton continued. "A five-minute speech on how many different ways your dog can shake a paw would be nothing short of painful. There's a great big world out there. Explore it, and then tell us about it." He looked around the room and smiled. "Okay, that's it. Stack your chairs and have a good night."

That evening, I sat at my computer and tried to think of a speech topic. First I Googled elementary speech topics. The computer spit out the ten most popular sites out of the thirty-three million it found. I clicked on the first one, which claimed to boast the top twenty-five speech topics. I laughed when I saw the number-five suggestion: "Funny Things My Pet Has Done."

Mr. Hamilton wouldn't like this site, I decided.

I stared at the keyboard waiting for inspiration.

Nothing.

Finally I began to Google names: Gordie Howe. Maurice Richard. Bobby Orr. Wayne Gretzky.

I clicked on different links and read the main parts of their bios. Every year I did a speech on a hockey player and I had to admit that they were never the most entertaining. Then I remembered something Scooter had said to me. I typed the name *Tim Horton*.

Tons of websites popped up. I wondered how many of my classmates even knew that he'd been a hockey player, and a good one too, judging by his stats.

I spent the rest of the night researching Tim Horton, and started to feel better about the assignment. I was about to shut down the computer when another idea popped into my mind. I typed in one more name: Scooter.

Google came back with a whole bunch of sites about scooters. It also found a German punk band named Scooter.

I decided to try one more time. I typed:

Scooter/Maple Leaf Gardens.

I nearly fell off my chair when the first hit was: *Whatever Happened to Scooter Murphy?*

The caption that appeared beside an icon for a video clip read: *Former Toronto Maple Leafs star Scooter Murphy hasn't been seen since Maple Leaf Gardens closed on February 13, 1999.*

My hand shook as I clicked on the icon. The screen moved to reveal a reporter standing in front of Maple Leaf Gardens. The date on the video showed *14/10/05.*

This is Randy Irving, the reporter said. *I'm here at Maple Leaf Gardens as we try to shed some light on the mystery of the disappearance of Scooter Murphy. Long-time Leafs fans will remember that Scooter played for the team in the 1950s and is best remembered for his incredible shot block in the overtime of game five of the 1951 Stanley Cup Final. The Montreal Canadiens were pressing furiously in Toronto's end. During a scramble, Leafs goalie Turk Broda was knocked out of his net. The puck bounced out to Hall of Famer Maurice Richard, who fired the puck at the empty net. Murphy came out of nowhere and dove in front of the Richard blast. The blocked shot preserved the tie, enabling Bill Barilko to score his famous cup-clinching goal on the very next shift.*

The next scene showed Mr. Irving standing in the front concourse of the Gardens, just a few steps away from where I had slept on my foam pad. As he continued with his tour of the Gardens, Irving carried on with his monologue.

Murphy was born in rural Ontario and grew up on a farm near Kitchener. As a seventeen-year-old in 1944, he lied about his age and enlisted in the Canadian military. That summer, he was wounded in the leg at Juno Beach as the Canadians fought heroically in the D-Day invasion of June 6th.

After the war, he returned to Canada where he began play-ing hockey for the St. Michael's College Majors. He signed with the Leafs and played his first full season with the big club in 1950. Scooter was never known as a goal scorer. He was known as a hard-working defensive winger.

Murphy's career came to an abrupt end in 1961 when he injured his knee during a game—the same leg that had been injured at Juno Beach. This was in an era before players' unions and collective bargaining agreements, and the Leafs quickly dropped him. Released by the team, and with little money to his name, Murphy was left to his own devices to survive. Scooter became a fixture in the neighbourhood around Maple Leaf Gardens. He worked odd jobs in the area and he could often be found on game nights selling broken sticks that the players and trainers would give him.

The video clip changed to footage of the last game played at the Gardens. I recognized former Leafs captain Darryl Sittler and Mats Sundin. Then suddenly, there was Scooter, walking out on the red carpet and waving at the fans. He was younger-looking and clean-shaven, but it was definitely the man who had befriended me.

The clip ended with Randy Irving back in front of the Gardens. He looked earnestly into the camera and said, "*Scooter Murphy attended the final game at Maple Leaf Gardens, on February 13, 1999, as an honoured guest of the team. Afterward, he simply vanished. He remains the greatest mystery in Toronto Maple Leafs' team history. To this day, many people are still asking: Whatever happened to Scooter Murphy?*

This has been Randy Irving reporting for The Hockey Trivia Show."

For the longest time, I just stared at the computer. I had spent all that time with Scooter and had only thought of him as an old, homeless person. Not only had he won the Stanley Cup, but he was a war hero. I was so ashamed of myself for not taking the time to really listen to Scooter. I began to remember pieces of our conversations, and realized that he'd been trying to tell me something.

I knew him, you know.

Who?

Tim Horton.

I pulled up Tim Hortons stats on the computer. Of course he knew him. They had been teammates.

I watched the video through one more time. As awful as I felt that I had misjudged Scooter so badly, I couldn't help smiling at the thought of Randy Irving walking around the Gardens, doing his report on Scooter Murphy, while Scooter was probably spying on him from the press box.

I was still smiling as I powered down the computer. Tim Horton seemed like an interesting person, but he wasn't nearly as fascinating as Scooter Murphy. For the first time ever, I was looking forward to presenting a speech.

CHAPTER TWENTY

The bell rang on Friday afternoon to signal the end of my first week back at school. I had quickly settled into my old routines, one of which included walking home with Sam. Each day we would stop at the same *Toronto Star* box, and I would jimmy the handle to get a free paper. Sam was impressed by my new-found skill, but I think she was even more impressed by the fact that after I took out the paper, I would deposit my money.

Living as a street kid had taught me some valuable lessons. First of all, I had learned how hard it is for people on the streets simply to survive. I had learned about the power of money. I had decided that if you can afford something, then you should take pride in paying for it. And I had become a news junkie. While reading the paper to Scooter each day, I had learned that there is a big, vast world out there filled with fascinating people and events. I was determined to learn as much as I could about all of it.

One day, after I bought my paper, I was chatting happily with Sam, thinking about whether I should try to hold her hand again, when I stopped dead in my tracks. There, blocking our path up the sidewalk, was my dad. I felt like I had been slammed into the boards in a hockey game. I couldn't speak, I couldn't move, I couldn't do anything.

Dad smiled. "Hi, Jake," he said.

I scrambled to regain my composure. "What do you want?" I challenged in what I hoped was a menacing voice.

Dad held out his hands like he was making a peace offering. "All I want to do is talk to you."

"Well, I don't want to listen, so get out of our way," I demanded.

Dad's smile vanished. "Jake," he tried again, "if you would just give me a chance."

"You beat me up!" I snapped. "All because I didn't fight some kid, or I hit a crossbar, or I didn't backcheck hard enough!"

He let out a frustrated grunt. "You just don't understand do you?" he yelled.

Sam and I both jumped, and took an immediate step backwards.

Seeing our reaction, Dad tried to calm himself. "I'm sorry," he said quickly.

"You need to leave me and Mom alone," I said. "I can't handle your freak-outs anymore."

Before he could say anything else, I took Sam's hand and we pushed past him and walked away.

We didn't say anything until we got to the corner where Sam would cut over to her house. The fear was starting to ebb when she broke the silence.

"I'm really sorry, Jake."

"What for?" I asked. "You didn't do anything wrong."

Sam shook her head. "I've always known that things were tough for you at home. I just never knew they were that bad."

"It's okay," I said.

"Do you want to talk about it?"

I laughed. "No, I don't."

"Okay," she said. "Then I guess this will have to do." She reached up and put her arms around my neck and kissed me.

Before I knew what was happening, it was over.

"See you tomorrow," she said, and then she turned for home.

As I watched her walk away, a smile broke across my face, and my dad was suddenly the last thing on my mind.

I decided not to tell Mom about my run-in with Dad, or my kiss from Sam. When the supper dishes were cleared, and she was busy doing some laundry, I sat down at the kitchen table and spread out the newspaper. I flipped through the front section, scanning headlines and looking at pictures, but nothing in particular caught my attention. I moved on to the Greater Toronto section. The headline on the front page leapt out at me:

MAPLE LEAF GARDENS TO UNDERGO
MASSIVE RENOVATION
by Miles Watson

Maple Leaf Gardens, the grand old hockey arena at the corner of Church and Carlton streets, will be undergoing a major facelift. Yesterday, Loblaws announced that it was joining forces with Ryerson University to convert the Gardens into an arena and sporting complex. It will also house a grocery store and shopping facilities.

The Toronto Maple Leafs played their last game at the Gardens on February 13, 1999. Since then, the arena has largely sat empty. Construction is scheduled to begin within the next few weeks.

Below the article were several photographs of the architectural drawings and I studied them carefully. I could tell that the changes were going to be massive. I knew, too, that Scooter couldn't possibly stay hidden during the construction. How long, exactly, before he'd be out on the street? *Maybe there will be more information online,* I thought.

I opened Mom's laptop, which she'd left on the table. She had a new message from someone named *HockeyStar27. Who's HockeyStar27?* I wondered.

Feeling very nosy, I clicked on the email.

Hi Becks,

I enjoyed our chat yesterday. Thanks for keeping me up to date on Jake. I'm glad he's settled back in with the team and at school. Maybe we can get together for dinner or a drink soon. I miss you.

Love, Jeff

I clicked off the email and just stared at the computer. What on earth was going on? Could Mom and Dad possibly be planning on getting back together?

"This day just keeps getting better and better," I muttered. Frustrated and confused, I forgot all about Scooter and his problems with the Gardens. I stood up and headed for my room. I flopped angrily down onto my bed and jammed my iPod earbuds into my ears. Then I tried unsuccessfully to clear my head with some really loud Jay-Z.

CHAPTER TWENTY-ONE

I woke Saturday morning with a pounding headache. I didn't know what to do about Mom and her sneaky emails with Dad, and on top of everything else, I was worried about Scooter. I thought that a shower might clear my head, but after fifteen minutes, though cleaner and smelling better, I was no closer to knowing what I needed to do.

Mom was sitting at the kitchen table, sipping a cup of tea and reading my newspaper. "Morning, honey."

I poured myself a bowl of cereal and sat down beside her. "Read the article about the Gardens?" I asked, pointing at the paper.

"No," she said, "I just sat down."

"It's going to be renovated—big shopping mall and a sports facility for Ryerson University."

"Uh-huh."

I wasn't even sure she was listening. "Construction starts soon," I said.

"Oh, yeah?" She sipped her tea.

I could feel my anger rising. "Yeah," I said. "What do you think will happen to Scooter?"

That got her attention. She put down her tea and looked at me. "I don't know," she said finally.

"I do. It means Scooter will be out on his butt. I need to help him."

"I don't see what you can do," Mom said.

"What do you mean? He's my friend. Let's go get him."

Mom sighed. "Be reasonable, Jake."

"Reasonable?" I challenged. "You just don't want to help him because he's homeless."

Mom stiffened, but I plowed ahead. "He's a war hero. He played for the Leafs. He saved my life when I was living on the streets." Suddenly I wasn't hungry anymore. I stomped out of the kitchen, turning around in the hallway and pointing my finger at her. "I'm gonna help him, and I'll do it with or without your help."

When I entered the rink that afternoon to take on the Don Mills Colts, I was still in a bad mood. Freddie was standing in the lobby, filling his face with arena fries. I grabbed a couple.

"Help yourself," he said as I stuffed the fries into my mouth.

"Thanks," I muttered.

"Everything okay?" he asked.

"Just peachy," I growled as I hustled off to the dressing room.

One thing I can say about being in a rotten mood is that it seems to go right to your legs. I was flying out there on the ice, and by the end of the first period I had already scored twice and we led 3–0. For the first time in my life, I hadn't looked to see where my mom was sitting during the game. But now that the goals had improved my mood, I scanned the group of North York parents. Everyone seemed to be there except Mom.

That's strange, I thought.

The second period got underway and I continued to search the crowd for her. The Colts goalie froze the puck for a whistle, and I stood up with Lyle and Joey to change our line. As I skated to the faceoff circle to the right of the Don Mills goalie, I happened to look up at the warm viewing area window behind the Plexiglas in the Don Mills end. Mom was standing behind the window and there, just visible in the corner, was Dad.

My good mood evaporated. "I don't believe it," I said to myself.

The linesman waved at me. "Come on, sixteen. Square up."

I looked around and realized that I was just standing in the middle of the faceoff circle. The linesman dropped the puck and the Don Mills centreman and I swatted away at it. The puck bounced to my right where Joey redirected a soft little deflection toward the net. Their goalie dropped to his knees and smothered the puck as the referee blew his whistle to stop the play. I was still a body-length away from the goalie when I heard the whistle, but I couldn't stop myself. As I skated past the goalie, I slashed him as hard as I could on the back of his catching hand. He let out a yelp and immediately swung at me with his stick. But the goalie was the least of my worries and I ignored his slash.

I spun around, and sure enough, two gigantic defencemen were barrelling toward me.

I swung as hard as I could and made contact with the first guy's facemask. I hit him so hard and so unexpectedly that I knocked him flat on his butt. His partner hit me from the side with a hard cross-check that caught me in the vulnerable spot on my arm between the bottom of my shoulder pad and the top of my elbow pad.

I howled as the pain shot through my arm.

I retaliated with a vicious two-handed slash, which struck him just above the ankle. A Don Mills forward tackled me to the ice, and I scrambled as hard as I could to fight him off, but I couldn't move. The rest of the players from both teams had jumped on top of us. I screamed and cursed until the referees finally managed to break apart the dog pile. When one of the linesmen finally got to me, I was completely exhausted. He helped me to my feet and I started to skate to the penalty box.

"Oh no, not you," the liney said, and he pushed me toward the exit. "You're done for this game."

Suddenly, I didn't feel as tough or as angry as I had a few minutes ago. I walked to our dressing room and waited for the trainer. He arrived with the room key and unlocked the door.

"You okay, Jake?" he asked.

I nodded.

"Sure you're not hurt?"

"I'm good."

He turned back to the door. "Madigan says not to go anywhere. He wants to talk with you." He pulled the door shut behind him.

"Terrific," I muttered to the back of the door.

By the time the team came into the room after the game, I was changed and sitting quietly by myself on the bench. A couple of guys congratulated me on my tough-guy routine, but most didn't say anything. It was like they knew something was wrong. Freddie sat down beside me and yanked off his goalie mask.

"Are you okay?" he asked.

I nodded.

"What happened?"

Even if I could have explained myself to Freddie, which I couldn't, I didn't have a chance. Madigan came in and clapped his hands for quiet.

"Okay, boys. The good news is we won, but I gotta say, that was a weird one. You guys hustle up and I'll see you at practice tomorrow. Jake, come see me."

Freddie looked like he was even more scared than I was.

"I'm sure it'll be fine," he said unconvincingly.

Madigan was waiting in the hallway for me.

"Follow me," he said.

He walked out into the arena and up into the empty seats. He sat down and gestured for me to take the seat beside him. For a while he seemed content to watch the Zamboni move slowly around the ice. Finally he said, "What was that all about?"

"I dunno."

"You don't know?" he challenged.

"I dunno," I repeated.

"Four minutes for slashing, four minutes for roughing, and a game misconduct and you *don't know*?"

All I could do was shrug.

"Jake, I asked Coach Whitney to check your stats. You had fourteen minutes in penalties all of last year. This year, you have taken three minor penalties so far. That's twenty minutes in penalties the last two years. Including your misconduct, you took *thirty-three* minutes in today's game."

I didn't know what he wanted me to say, so I just continued to stare at the Zamboni.

"Oh, come on, Jake. The least you can do is tell me what set you off. Did you get hacked?"

I shook my head.

"Speared?"

"No."

"Did somebody say something to you?"

Suddenly, my eyes were brimming with tears.

"It's okay, Jake," Madigan said. "You're not in trouble. I just want to know what set you off."

As I wiped my eyes with the back of my hand, I could see the concern on his face.

"They were watching the game together," I said.

"Huh?" Madigan sounded confused. "Who?"

"My folks. They were watching the game together."

"Ah!" Madigan exclaimed. "I take it that kind of upset you."

I nodded, wiped at my eyes and snorted all at the same time. "I guess so."

Madigan smiled kindly. "Well, you know what? I don't blame you for being upset," he said. "You've had a tough time this year, and your dad has been pretty rough on you. Thanks for telling me the truth, Jake."

He stood up and was about to head back to the dressing room. "And Jake, if you ever need someone to talk to, I'd be happy to listen. You don't need to run away from your problems or attempt to destroy half of the Don Mills team by yourself."

I tried to smile. "Thanks, Coach."

Mom was standing with Freddie's mom out in the lobby, but Dad didn't seem to be around.

"I better get him home for dinner," Mom said to Mrs. Talbot, tipping her head toward me. "See you tomorrow, Janet."

On the drive home, I decided I had to say something. "I didn't see you sitting with the other moms," I said. "Where were you?"

"Oh, I was cold, so I decided to watch the game from the warm viewing area."

"All by yourself?" I tried to study her out of the corner of my eye.

"I didn't mind. I was more worried about staying warm than I was about socializing. And by the way, what on earth got into you today?"

"Guy speared me," I said.

"Well, I've never seen you that angry in a game before, and I've got to say, I don't like you playing like that. Are you all right now?"

"I'm fine." It was the first time that I could remember lying to my mother. But it was also the first time that I knew that she was lying to me too.

CHAPTER TWENTY-TWO

The last couple of weeks leading up to the Quebec Peewee Tournament passed by in a blur. I went to school, worked on my speech, played hockey, and walked home from school every day with Sam. After our run-in with my dad on the sidewalk, I'd given up trying to hide stuff from her. It was so nice to have someone to talk to. I told her everything, starting with the first time my dad hit me way back in Novice. I told her about knowing how my folks were talking and probably planning to get back together. I told her about Scooter; about how he protected me when I ran away. About the fact that the Gardens was going to be renovated any day now, and how I still didn't know how to help him.

"He can't stay with me—my mom would lose her mind," I said one afternoon.

"Have you ever thought of a seniors' home?" Sam asked.

Scooter could never afford a seniors' home, I thought. "Uh, not exactly," I answered.

"There's one just around the corner from your place," she said. "Pine something, or oak or maple. I forget what it's called. Let's go have a look." She took my hand, and even though I knew it was a wasted trip, I wasn't going to let go.

We went down a quiet residential street. The road meandered lazily back towards the north and ended in a large cul-de-sac. One side of the street was occupied by a long, impressive complex, which was tucked in behind a stand of tall pines. It was made up of a series of one-storey units that branched off in all directions. The sign out front announced the place as the WHISPERING PINES RETIREMENT CENTRE.

I snorted. "Original name."

"Give it a chance," Sam said.

Inside, we found a large front foyer filled with couches and easy chairs and paintings of landscapes hanging on the walls. A middle-aged woman sat at the reception desk.

"May I help you?" she asked pleasantly.

Never really comfortable around strangers, I immediately froze. Sam rescued me. "We'd just like to look around if that's okay."

The lady was clearly not used to random children showing up to look around. Sam hurriedly added, "We're supposed to do some volunteer hours for our school and we thought . . ." She began to struggle with her story.

". . . maybe we'd like to do them here," I added.

The woman's face broke into a gigantic smile. "That is a wonderful idea. Come, come." She rummaged through her desk, then leaned across and clipped a visitor's pass onto each of our coats. We had to sign the guest book and she told us where we could and couldn't go.

"Uh, how much does it cost for a person to stay here?" I asked.

The lady looked surprised by the question.

"It's for my assignment. On the seniors' home," I said.

"Oh," she said. "Well, it varies for each person. You know, private room, double room, that sort of thing, but it starts at about two thousand dollars a month."

I felt my stomach drop. Man, that was a lot of money.

Sam told the lady that we'd only be a few minutes. Then she grabbed my hand and said, "Let's go."

She dragged me down a hallway and around a corner until we were out of sight of the perky lady at reception. Sam slowed down and whispered, "What do you want to do?"

"Take a quick look around, I guess," I said. "It would be weird if we just left."

We came to a large open area. It was bright and cheery with lots of windows and more easy chairs. Two elderly men were playing a game of pool. When they saw us they stopped long enough to wave.

Around another corner we came upon a room that was full of card tables. It buzzed with conversation. "I think we've stumbled across some sort of tournament," Sam said.

A lady at the nearest table looked up from her cards. "Are you dears looking for someone?"

Sam shook her head and smiled back. "No, we're just visiting."

"Oh, how nice."

I wanted to move on, but Sam gestured at all the tables. "So, what are you doing?"

"Euchre tournament," the lady said. "Every Wednesday afternoon. We play just for bragging rights. Winners get to gloat for a week." She looked across the table at her partner and smiled. "What do you think, Phyllis? Maybe we'll win this week, eh?"

"We never win," Phyllis grumbled miserably.

I said, "I bet this will be your week. Good luck." Then I looked at Sam and said, "We'd better get going."

"Come back and visit anytime," the friendly woman said.

We promised that we would. As we were leaving, I heard Phyllis scolding our new friend. "Edna, we'll never win if you don't pay attention."

On our way home, I thought about how Scooter could be friendly like Edna and grumpy like Phyllis. He'd love that pool table. I started to see how he might just fit in at Whispering Pines—if only it wasn't so impossibly expensive.

CHAPTER TWENTY-THREE

We had only a few games left before our trip to Quebec City when we took on Mississauga. They were a good team, but we dominated them in both ends of the rink. When they took a shot, Freddie would turn it aside. When we got a chance, more often than not it found the back of the net. I had another strong game, posting a goal and two assists in a 6–1 victory.

After the game, I found Coach Madigan at the canteen, ordering a coffee. I cleared my throat. "You know you said I could talk to you, right?"

Madigan picked up his bag of sweaters and water bottles, and gestured with his chin to a quiet spot in the corner. "What's up?" he asked once we'd moved there, dropping his stuff on the floor.

"Coach, I was wondering if you would be able to tell me how much money I raised this year."

Madigan raised a quizzical eyebrow. This was clearly not the heart-to-heart he was expecting. "Well, we've raised about eighteen hundred dollars per player. Do you mind my asking why you want to know?"

I ignored that question and asked another. "If I sat out of the tournament, could I have the money I raised for myself?"

Madigan shook his head. "I don't think so, Jake. The money was raised so that you could go to Quebec. Are you going to tell me what you need the money for?"

"It's a long story," I said.

Madigan leaned back against the arena wall and sipped his coffee. "I've got time."

"I want to give the money to a friend," I said slowly.

"Do you owe someone money? Oh no! Are you on drugs?" Madigan was really beginning to panic.

I tried not to laugh. "No, I'm not on drugs."

"Listen, kiddo, why don't you start at the beginning."

So, I told him about Scooter, about the Gardens renovation, and about Sam's idea to put Scooter in a seniors' home. Madigan listened carefully and didn't interrupt.

Finally, I explained that if I could get the eighteen hundred dollars, it would buy Scooter one month in a seniors' home. Then we'd have to figure something else out.

Madigan was stunned. "Do you mean to tell me that you know where Scooter Murphy is?"

"Yes."

"*The* Scooter Murphy?"

I smiled and nodded.

"Scooter Murphy, the guy who assisted on Bill Barilko's winner in '51, then disappeared ten years ago, never to be seen again?"

"That's him," I said. "But he didn't assist on the goal. He blocked a shot to preserve the tie. Barilko scored on the next shift."

Madigan shook his head. "Son, I'm the biggest Leafs fan in the world. I'll bet you a Coke that he assisted on the winner." Then his face turned serious. "Jake, even if you get Scooter into a home for one month, then what will you do?"

I had to admit I didn't have a clue.

Madigan began pacing. "Nope, there's got to be a better way. Let's think about this. There's MLSE."

"What's that?" I asked.

"MLSE is short for Maple Leaf Sports & Entertainment. They might have some ideas. What else? What else?" he said more to himself than to me. "We could go to the radio stations and the newspapers. Let people know about Scooter's story. I bet people would donate money." He looked at me, pleased with his ideas. "Jake, there's no way you're missing the Quebec Peewee Tournament. I'll do what I can to help you raise money for Scooter, but you *will* play in Quebec."

"Thanks, Coach," I said.

With all the help I'd had from Scooter, Reverend Pete, Sam, and now Coach Madigan, I felt like I wasn't completely on my own for the first time in a long time. Maybe we could make this work after all.

As I listened to my classmates deliver their speeches, I felt like a prisoner awaiting execution. I wanted to stick my tongue out at Susie Reed, the class keener, who, with the fakest smile I'd ever seen, delivered her presentation on the proper way to paddle a canoe.

Give me a break, I thought as I tuned out Susie's perky babble.

Watching a little guy named Ben deliver his speech helped to calm me down. *This poor guy is even more nervous than I am,* I thought. His hands were shaking so much that he had trouble reading his cue cards. At the end, I even raised my hand and asked a question during the Q&A to help him out.

"What made you choose that topic?" I asked. An easy one.

Ben smiled gratefully. "My mom suggested it," he said. When Ben was finished being interrogated, he returned to his seat with a look on his face that said "I don't have to do that again for another year."

"Jake? You ready?" Mr. Hamilton asked.

I pushed my chair back.

"Good luck," Sam whispered.

"Thanks."

At the front of the room, I looked down at my cue cards and took a deep breath.

"Charlie Conacher, Johnny Bower, Tim Horton, Darryl Sittler, Mats Sundin." I looked up briefly. Mr. Hamilton was always saying to look at the audience.

"Billy Bishop, Andrew Mynarski, Isaac Brock, Arthur Currie, Ernest 'Smokey' Smith.

"What do these men have in common? Well, the first group is made up of famous Toronto Maple Leafs, and the second group is a list of Canadian war heroes. Mr. Hamilton and fellow classmates, I would like to talk to you today about a man who played for the Leafs and is also a war hero. His name is Scooter Murphy."

I took another glance at the class and was relieved to see that the kids seemed to be interested. *So far, so good.* I told them about Scooter's time in the military and his knee injury during the war, and then, of course, I talked about his career with the Leafs.

"Now some of you may be thinking this guy sounds really cool. Why haven't I heard of him? The reason you haven't heard of him is probably that Scooter is a homeless person."

There was a collective gasp from the class, which I found particularly satisfying.

"Earlier this year, I ran away from home. To make a long story short, I took the subway into Toronto and ended up breaking into Maple Leaf Gardens."

I hadn't meant to be funny, but a few of the kids laughed softly.

"It was while I took shelter in the Gardens that I met Scooter. He has been living in the building ever since it was shut down after the Leafs moved to the Air Canada Centre. For over ten years, Scooter has survived by trying to stay warm in the Gardens and relying on the charity of good people like Reverend Peter Ambrose at the Christian Charity Soup Kitchen. Scooter has long, scraggly hair and this wild beard, and, man, does he smell. But you know what? I smelled too. In fact, after ten days of living on the streets, I absolutely reeked."

More laughter. The speech was going well, and now I was ready to wrap it up.

"I guess what I'm trying to say is that I've learned a lot this year. I've learned that you never judge a book by its cover. And I've learned that we all need heroes and role models. My hero is a homeless man named Scooter Murphy. I hope that you all get a chance to meet your hero someday. Just remember that he may be wearing an old ratty jacket and eating a grilled cheese sandwich at a soup kitchen." I took one last look at my classmates and let out a long sigh. I was pleased with my effort. "Thanks for listening."

To my surprise, almost every kid in the class raised his or her hand to ask a question.

"Where is Scooter now?" Susie Reed asked.

"He's still living at the Gardens, as far as I know," I answered.

The class continued to fire questions at me. I was feeling really good because Mr. Hamilton had said that the sign of a good speech was how many questions it generated. I was still thinking about this when Ben raised his hand.

Ben never raises his hand, I thought.

"Yes, Ben?"

"Why did you run away, Jake?"

Mr. Hamilton jumped to my defence from the back of the room. "Jake, you don't have to answer that one. Okay, folks, let's get ready to move on. Sam, I think you're next."

"Mr. Hamilton?"

"Yes, Jake?"

"I think I should answer Ben's question."

When I was writing my speech I thought about how no one had asked me why I left. But I knew Ben wasn't the only one who wondered. And I knew what I wanted to say.

I looked around the room at my friends. Some of them I'd

known since kindergarten. "I know that some of you were really worried about me when I just vanished like that. You see, my dad . . . well, my dad thinks that I'm going to be a great hockey player someday. And his way of getting the best out of me was to push really hard, you know?" The first tear ran down my cheek before I could register the horrifying fact that I was about to cry in front of my classmates. "I was never good enough, and I'd get hit or punched, and it just got really tough to take, so one night I decided I'd had enough and I took off. But things are better now."

Sam flashed me an everything's-okay smile. I looked at my other classmates and shrugged. "I guess that's it. Now you know."

I went back to my desk and sat down. The room was completely quiet.

Then Susie Reed, of all people, began to clap. And then Stilts and Ben, and soon the whole class was clapping.

As Sam stood up to deliver her speech, she whispered, "That took a lot of guts, Jake."

Even more than you know, I thought. I felt like I'd just sprinted across the catwalk from my worst nightmares.

At recess, Sam and I walked across the soccer field to the fence that ran around the perimeter of the schoolyard. The fence met the school at the back of the gymnasium, and for some reason didn't butt into the corner of the gym, but ran past it and out toward the road. It created a small alley about a metre and a half wide. Kids would go there when they didn't want to be seen by the suspicious eyes of the yard-duty teacher. Most of our teachers would just stand in the middle of the yard and drink their coffee. From that vantage point, they couldn't see around the edge of the gym.

As we entered the alley, Sam was so scared she was shaking.

"Relax, we haven't done anything wrong." Then, just to get a rise out of her, I added, "Yet."

"Jacob Dumont, if you get me into trouble . . ."

"All you have to do is keep a lookout. If you see a teacher, just walk away. If I get caught, I'll deal with it." I knew that what I was about to do was a fairly minor infraction. Using a cell phone without permission would probably get me a couple of recess detentions, but to Sam, who had never been in trouble in her life, we might as well have been getting ready to knock off a bank.

Sam peered around the corner, on alert for any sign of a teacher.

"Sam," I said.

She jumped and spun around.

"Your phone?"

"Right." She handed it to me. "Make it quick."

I had memorized the phone number and a bunch of other stuff that I needed, and now I dialled quickly. A voice came on the other end.

"Maple Leaf Sports & Entertainment, how may I direct your call?"

"Extension 4200, please."

I listened to a series of clicks and then a man picked up.

"Theodore Lennox."

"Hi," I said. "You're the head of the Leafs public relations department, right?"

"That's right, how can I help you?"

"I'd like to talk to you about Scooter Murphy."

CHAPTER TWENTY-FOUR

That night when Mom and I sat down together for dinner, I had no appetite and barely picked at my food. It had been quite a day. My speech had gone really well, I had talked to Theodore Lennox about Scooter, and I'd also been caught using a cell phone by Mrs. Harris, the yard-duty teacher. I tried to talk my way out of it, but she had just sneered that sucked-on-a-lemon sneer of hers and sent me to the office.

"How was school today?" Mom asked.

Her voice cut through the silence of the room and startled me. "Okay, I guess," I said, recovering quickly. "I gave my speech today."

"How'd it go?"

"I think it went really well."

"That's good. Anything else happen?"

I dropped my eyes and looked at my plate. Busted.

"I got caught using a cell phone."

Mom frowned. "I know. Ms. O'Toole called me. I hear you have detention tomorrow."

"Yeah, I do," I admitted.

"Whose phone?"

"Sam's."

"And who were you calling?"

"I called Maple Leaf Sports & Entertainment."

Mom looked startled. "You did what?"

"I called and talked to the director of public relations and I told him that I know where Scooter Murphy is."

Mom leaned forward and put her head into her hands. "When Ms. O'Toole said you were using a cell phone, I thought you were calling Freddie or some other friend." She shook her head. "I can't believe you did that, Jake."

"What's the big deal?" I demanded.

"What's the big deal?" she echoed. "It's a big deal. It's a big deal because . . ." She seemed to be at a loss for words.

She doesn't know, I thought. And that's when I went from being scared about being in trouble to being just plain old angry.

"I told you I was gonna help him," I said firmly. "What's the big deal?"

"It is a big deal!" was all she could say.

"Yeah, and you don't know why. Well, let me tell you why!" I couldn't help raising my voice. "You're afraid of him! You're afraid of him, and you've never even met him."

Mom's eyes widened, but she didn't deny it. For years I'd crept around my house trying not to draw any attention to myself. But now the words were flowing out of me.

"I don't get you, Mom," I shouted. "Unlike you, Scooter did

everything he could to keep me safe, and you're scared of *him*!"

"Jacob Dumont," Mom said. "Don't you ever take that tone with me again!"

"Or else what? You gonna beat me up too?" I shot back. "Or are you gonna call Dad to pop over and maybe he can smack me around a bit."

"How dare you!" Mom yelled.

"Oh, you are such a liar!"

Mom looked like she'd been slapped.

"I saw that email from Dad," I said. "Oh, Becks, I miss you," I sang in a loud, sarcastic voice.

"And I saw you with him at the game the other day. You said you were cold, but you were with Dad and you *lied* to me."

Mom raised a trembling hand to her face and her eyes began to fill with tears. "Oh, Jake," she said. "I'm so sorry. What you must have been thinking of me the last few days."

I wasn't about to soften because of her tears. "You gonna let him back in the house?"

"No, Jake," she said. "Your father and I have both agreed that he shouldn't come back anytime soon. But he's got a therapist who's trying to help him with his anger. That's what we were talking about at the rink."

"Oh," I said quietly. I could see the hurt in her eyes, and for the first time I thought of him not as my dad, but as her husband. "Do you still love him?" I asked.

Mom nodded. "Yeah, I do."

"Do you want to get back together?"

Mom gave a little shrug. "Some days I do. But I promise that neither Dad nor I will do anything without running it by you first."

How can you go from being so mad at someone one second to feeling so sorry for them the next? I wondered.

"I'm sorry," I said.

She wiped her eyes. "Me too, Jake." Then she tried to smile. "So what did the guy from the Leafs say?"

I tried to clear my head. "He said that he'd be willing to meet me, if I was able to prove that Scooter really is who he says he is."

"Well, that's good, isn't it?" she asked.

"I don't know. I'm not sure he has a driver's licence or anything."

Mom smiled. "Well, Jake, you've proven yourself to be a very loyal friend. I'm sure you'll think of something."

The next morning a piece of paper was waiting for me on the kitchen table beside my cereal bowl.

"What's this?" I asked Mom.

"Read it," she said.

Department of National Defence
Enlisted Personnel Search
ID # 8736542
Private Edward Murphy
DOB: February 12, 1927, Kitchener Ontario
Enlisted on Active Service: January 7, 1944
Princess Patricia's Light Infantry
Honourable Discharge from Active Service: January 27, 1946

I looked back at Mom, dumbstruck. "I don't understand," I said.

Mom shrugged. "I couldn't sleep last night. You certainly gave me a lot to think about, Jake. And the more I thought of it, the more I realized I needed to help you. I found it on the Department of Defence website."

I read the paper again. "This could help. Thank you."

"There's something else I should do too, Jake."

"What's that?" I asked.

"I think it's time I met Scooter."

CHAPTER TWENTY-FIVE

Early on Saturday morning, I directed Mom through the streets of downtown Toronto. As soon as our van turned down Wood Street, I knew that we had trouble. The doors across the back of the arena were wide open and workers were bustling about.

"I didn't know they were starting yet," I said.

Mom was gripping the steering wheel in both hands. "Looks awfully busy, Jake. Maybe this isn't such a good idea."

Before she could try to talk me out of it, I grabbed the door handle and jumped out. "Be right back, Mom."

Once I was certain my mom was the only one watching me, I ran toward the old iron gate. Sure enough, the chain was still just wrapped around the fence. Quietly, I removed it and opened the gate, slipping into the back alley. I climbed the stairs of the fire escape and was so relieved to see Scooter's skate lace hanging through the door jamb. I pulled on the lace and was able to open the door just enough to wedge my fingers into the opening. When I stepped inside, I found a new problem. The interior of the Gardens was brightly illuminated, which would make sneaking into the press box that much more difficult. I cautiously moved to the front of the concession stand, and was about to step out into the hallway when I heard voices. I ducked down behind the counter and waited. Two people were talking nearby. Their voices got louder as they passed my hiding spot and then faded as they moved on.

When I was sure that the hallway was empty, I went around the front of the concession stand, peeked into the hall, and took a quick scan in both directions.

Empty. It's now or never.

I sprinted down the hall. My footfalls echoed loudly as I grabbed the escalator, spun around its base without breaking stride, and sped up. I took the escalator stairs two at a time and didn't stop until I reached the upper concourse. Then I ran toward an archway that led into the highest section of seats—the greys. I stopped and listened. When I didn't hear any pursuers, I slowly made my way forward.

The vast expanse of the Gardens opened up before me. Fifteen or twenty workers were milling about on the arena floor. They didn't appear to be doing much of anything, but if one of them glanced up into the greys, I would be spotted. I was just thinking that I had no way of getting to the press box undetected, when another person walked out onto the arena floor. By the way the rest of the workers began to scurry in all directions, I could tell that the man must be the boss. I didn't hesitate. I slipped up the stairs and vanished into the top row of the greys. Up here it was too dark to be seen from ice level.

I moved quickly, but cautiously. I was in an unexplored part of the arena. When I was living in the Gardens, I had never gone up into the press box. Scooter had never invited me, and besides, I couldn't have made it across the catwalk. Now I had no choice. I came to the old, rickety-looking walkway that stretched from the last row of the greys out to the backside of the press box.

Scooter walks across this thing?

I grabbed onto the railing, stepped up onto the walkway, and immediately lost my nerve. The catwalk seemed to stretch endlessly, creeping higher and higher above the arena floor. The drop from the press box to the concrete below had to be five or six storeys. All my nightmares of falling to my death came rushing back to me.

Come on, you can do this, I told myself. *They were only dreams.*

Before my legs completely turned to jelly, I forced myself to take one step.

"*Unngh,*" I whimpered. "I can't do this." I could see the whites of my knuckles as I squeezed the railing. My legs were shaking and all I could hear were the scared-animal sounds coming out of my throat. Then suddenly, I heard voices. Good ones. Bad ones. And every time I heard a voice, my feet moved.

There'll be no TV until you score again! Step.

Crossbar and in baby! Step.

Scouts want toughness! Step.

Merry Christmas, Rebecca! Step.

You should have fought that kid! Step.

That took a lot of guts, Jake! Step.

My breath was pounding in my ears and my legs were heavier than they'd ever been in any hockey game, but I could see the edge of the press box getting closer. I was half laughing, half crying as I stepped off into the press box. And now the voice I heard in my head was my own.

I did it!

I moved over to one of the large windows that overlooked the rink and studied my surroundings. The press box was actually a series of small cubicles that ran the length of the Gardens. They all seemed to be empty, but when I peeked my head into the last one, there he was. He was crouched low, peering out the window, only his head above the glass. To avoid startling him, I called out quietly to my friend.

He spun around, a look of terror on his face. When he saw that it was me, he let out a deep breath. "Jake," he said, "you scared me."

"Sorry about that."

Scooter crawled away from the window, then stood and walked to a decrepit easy chair in the corner. He sat down.

"Well," he said, "come on in."

I took a quick look around his room. In addition to the easy chair, there was an old cot with a sleeping bag wedged into the corner. Some clothes lay strewn about on the floor. And that appeared to be about it for Scooter's worldly possessions. I stood in the centre of the room not knowing what to do next.

"Well, Jake," Scooter said. "I'd offer you a seat, but I don't have one."

I smiled. "That's okay."

Scooter looked out the press box window. "You know what's going on out there?" he asked.

"Yeah. The building's going to hold a new rink, a sports complex, and a huge shopping development."

"It'll be nice to watch hockey again," Scooter said.

"Scooter," I said gently. "I don't think you understand. They're going to find you up here. It's only a matter of time."

"They've never found me before," Scooter argued. "Movie shoots, television shoots—no one has ever found me."

"I've seen the plans," I said. "The entire building is being changed all the way up to the roof."

Scooter's confident expression slipped from his face as the reality of what I was saying set in.

"They will find you," I repeated.

"But this is my home."

"I know, but it's time to leave."

Scooter stood up and began pacing back and forth in the small room. "I can't leave, Jake. I've got nowhere else to go, and I sure can't survive on the streets."

"You've got a place," I said. "You're going to come home with me."

Scooter shook his head. "No, I couldn't do that."

"Sure you could. It would only be for a while, until we can find you another place."

"What about your folks?"

"My dad isn't in the house anymore," I said.

"Oh," Scooter said. "I'm sorry."

"That's okay." Then I brightened. "My mom is looking forward to having you stay with us."

Okay, this was a bit of a lie. If I couldn't figure out a way to get him into the Whispering Pines soon, I had no idea how long Mom would let him stay.

"They won't find me," he repeated. "I'll take my chances."

I sighed, frustrated. "Scooter," I said. "Mr. Murphy."

Scooter stared at me. "What did you say?"

I stared back at my friend. "Your name is Scooter Murphy. You played for the Leafs. You won the Stanley Cup. You were wounded at Juno Beach."

"How'd you find all that out?" he asked.

"I researched you on the Internet. Scooter, you were here, at Maple Leaf Gardens, on February 13, 1999, and then you vanished. People have been wondering what happened to you for over ten years."

Scooter puffed out his chest ever so slightly. "They have?"

"Yeah, they have. Come on, let's go home. You don't deserve to be hiding in this rickety old box."

Scooter stared down again at the arena floor, deep in thought. Finally, he turned back from the window and looked at me.

"Okay," he said. "Let's go."

As Scooter and I stepped off the bottom step of the fire escape, Mom got out of the van. She was holding her hands rigidly at her sides. I had to look away because I was afraid that I would laugh out loud. *Man, she is completely terrified*, I thought.

"Scooter Murphy, I'd like you to meet my mom, Rebecca Dumont."

I tried to picture him the way a stranger would; the way I had before I got to know him. He had a wild mane of white beard and long, scraggly hair, and he was definitely fresh.

Scooter smiled at Mom and held out his hand.

"It is a pleasure to meet you, Mrs. Dumont," he said quietly.

Finally, Mom reached out and shook Scooter's hand. "It's nice to meet you too, Scooter," she said nervously. "And I want to thank you for taking care of Jake when he was living in the Gardens."

Way to go, Mom.

I had never been more proud of her than I was at that moment.

CHAPTER TWENTY-SIX

Mom and I took Scooter home and set him up in the guest room. We spent most of that first night sitting around talking. At least Mom and Scooter talked. I mostly listened, and the more they talked, the more Mom relaxed. By the time they figured out that Scooter may have been in the same regiment as Mom's grandpa, they were talking like old friends. The most exciting part of the evening was when Scooter told us a story about how he had lost his dog tags one night during the war. He laughed softly as he admitted he'd lost them not during action in France, but after a night of drinking in a British pub.

"I was always worried about losing them again, so I did this." He pulled up his sleeve. "It's kind of faded, but I think you can still see it."

I went over to him and saw a serial number tattooed on his forearm. I leaned in close and squinted. "Looks like an eight," I said.

"8–7–3–6–5–4–2! Private Murphy, Princess Pat's Light Infantry, reporting for duty—sir!" Scooter said. "Goodness, it's amazing what you remember. I haven't said that for over sixty years."

"That's incredible, Scooter!" I said, looking over at Mom. She was smiling and nodding at me knowingly. "Scooter, I want to hear some more of your stories, but I just need to check something first. I'll be right back."

"Don't be long, Jake. I got lots more good stories," he said, and his eyes twinkled mischievously.

8–7–3–6–5–4–2, I repeated to myself as I scooted down the hall to my room. 8–7–3–6–5–4–2. I pulled out the piece of paper that Mom had printed off for me with Scooter's military information. As I scanned the page, the number jumped out at me: 8–7–3–6–5–4–2.

On Sunday morning Mom took Scooter and me out for an old-fashioned glazed. Later, we stopped at some stores and got Scooter some new clothes and a nice red parka.

"One more stop," Mom said.

When Scooter came out of the barber shop, I barely recognized him. His hair and beard were both neatly trimmed. He smiled shyly at me.

"What do you think, Jake?"

"I think you look awesome, Scooter."

Later that afternoon the three of us walked into the arena for my game against Pickering. Freddie was standing in the lobby, gorging on arena fries. I said goodbye to Mom and Scooter and walked to the dressing room with Freddie.

"Is that your grandpa?" he asked.

I stole a fry. As I stuffed it into my mouth I said, "Sort of."

"Sort of? How can he sort of be your grandpa?" Freddie asked.

"'Cause, we're more like friends than grandpa and grandson."

This seemed to satisfy Freddie. As he leaned on the dressing room door, I reached over and stole another fry.

Scooter was really excited about the game even though it was only Peewee and not the NHL. He talked about my three goals most of the way home. He finally seemed to be slowing down just as we were getting back to our neighbourhood. I turned around in my seat and said, "Scooter, can I ask you a question?"

"Sure!" he said brightly.

"How would you feel if I told some people about you?"

"What do you mean?"

"I dunno. I guess I don't understand why you never told anyone who you are. You know, like Reverend Pete, people at the soup kitchen."

He had a sad look on his face. "I'm not really proud of how I've . . . how I've ended up."

I studied his face, and I could see the embarrassment and shame that it held. It was weird, but in my own way, I understood about shame.

"You know, Jake," Scooter continued. "When I hurt my knee and I couldn't play anymore, at least I could always find work. Not much, but odd jobs, enough for food and a place to stay. I had a tiny little basement apartment just around the corner from the Gardens. But then one day, I woke up and I was an old man. No one would hire me anymore. It wasn't long before I ran out of money. I lost my apartment just before the Leafs' last game at the Gardens. The night of the final game, I just did what I had to do to stay warm. Next thing I knew, ten years had gone by."

I wondered if there was more to the story, but had a feeling that was as much as he wanted to say. "I'm sorry, Scooter. Let's forget about it, okay?"

To my surprise, he shook his head. "Jake, if you want to talk to people about me, you go right ahead. Just remember one thing. I won't talk to anyone else about this. You're the first person I've ever told."

I looked back at him and smiled. "I appreciate that, Scooter."

I called Theodore Lennox again, and he sounded skeptical when I told him that Scooter Murphy was living at my house, but he did agree to come over that night.

After a quick dinner, Mom and I scurried about, cleaning up, while Scooter sat nervously in the easy chair and watched us. At exactly 7 p.m., our doorbell rang.

"I got it!" I yelled.

Two men stood at the door. Both were dressed in expensive suits. I recognized the man on the left from the MLSE website photo. Theodore Lennox. The man on the right also looked familiar, but I couldn't place his face.

"You must be Jake," Theodore Lennox said, holding out his hand.

I shook his hand and said, "Thank you for coming, Mr. Lennox."

He smiled. "Call me Ted." Then he turned to the other man and said, "Jake, I hope you don't mind, but I took the liberty of inviting my friend Colby to come along."

Suddenly, I knew who he was. "You're Colby Tempest!" I said excitedly. "You used to play for the Leafs!"

Colby laughed. "Oh, we got a Leafs fan here, Ted. I didn't think anyone knew who I was, even when I played."

I liked Colby Tempest instantly. He had a kind face and friendly eyes. In fact, he kind of reminded me of Scooter.

Just then, Mom appeared behind us.

"Hello," she said. "I'm Rebecca. It looks like Jake forgot to invite you in." She motioned with her hand. "Please, come on in."

We led them into the living room where Scooter was already seated. He stood hesitantly when the two men entered.

"Scooter Murphy," I said. "This is Ted Lennox and Colby Tempest."

They shook hands and then we each took a seat. Although everyone was smiling, the room felt tense.

As if he was reading my mind, Ted Lennox began to speak. "Sir, I apologize if I sound doubtful, but MLSE does need proof that you are Scooter Murphy. It's no disrespect to you, it's just that, well . . . the Leafs can't announce that you've been found without evidence."

"I understand," Scooter said. "Team's having a tough year, eh?"

Ted's face was grave. "We can't afford a public relations mistake. However, if we can demonstrate that you truly are Scooter Murphy, then that could be a real boost to our season."

"How could I possibly be a boost to your season?" Scooter asked.

Ted looked uncomfortable. "If you don't mind, can we verify your identity before we get into that?"

"Scooter doesn't have any ID," I told them. "But we do have this." I got up and handed Ted the printout from the Department of National Defence.

Mr. Lennox looked at it and his eyebrows arched slightly. He handed the piece of paper to Colby.

"What do you think?" he asked.

Colby said, "This is definitely information about Scooter Murphy. But how do we know that the man sitting here matches the information on this paper?"

"Because," I said. I motioned for Scooter to stand up. "Show them, Scooter."

Scooter went over to the two men and pulled up his sleeve. For the longest time their eyes darted from Scooter's tattoo to the piece of paper and back again. The tension was broken when Colby Tempest jumped up.

"I don't believe it!" he exclaimed. "You really *are* Scooter Murphy!"

Ted Lennox rose, too, and extended his hand.

"Mr. Murphy, please forgive our skepticism. We just had to be sure."

Scooter laughed good-naturedly. "So now that you know who I am, why don't you two fellas tell me why you're here?"

Ted and Colby still seemed kind of shocked that they'd really found Scooter Murphy. Ted shrugged and said, "Why don't I go first."

Scooter sat back down in the easy chair and smiled patiently.

"Scooter, the Toronto Maple Leafs would like to have you drop the puck at an opening faceoff to one of our games this year."

"Oh, Scooter, that's wonderful," Mom said, beaming.

"I'd drop the puck to start the game?" Scooter asked, sounding confused.

Lennox smiled. "It would be a ceremonial puck that you would drop before the game between the two team captains."

"What kind of ceremony?" Scooter asked.

"Why, to welcome you back, of course. Scooter, you've been gone a long time, and you did win the Stanley Cup."

"That seems like an awful fuss just for me," Scooter said.

Lennox shook his head. "It gets better, Scooter. We're talking a limo ride to the game, front-row seats and a big introduction on the Jumbotron."

"Yes!" I yelled. "Can I come too?"

Scooter, who looked like he was still completely baffled by the whole concept, just shrugged.

"Of course you'll come," Lennox said. "Your Mom as well."

"I've never been to a Leafs game," I said.

"It's been a long time for me too," Scooter said.

"Well," Lennox said. "That's what I meant when I said you could be a boost to our season. Bringing you back at the ACC would really give our fans something to cheer about." Then he looked over at Colby. "Now, Colby has the *really* important news."

"More important than a Leafs game?" Scooter and I both asked simultaneously, which made us laugh.

Lennox smiled. "Oh, yes. This is much more important. Go ahead, Colby."

"Mr. Murphy, I don't think that I told you where I worked when we were introduced. I work for the NHLPA."

"What's that?" Scooter asked.

"It stands for the National Hockey League Players' Association. It's a union that the NHL players belong to. They look out for each other. After Jake phoned Ted the other day to say that he knew where you were, Ted thought that the union should be involved, so he phoned me. I did some research and made some phone calls. Do you know how many games you played in the NHL?"

Scooter shrugged. "No idea."

Colby smiled. "Well, I do. You played five hundred and seventy-three games. Today, with the union, an NHL player qualifies for a full pension if he plays four hundred games. Now, you played in the days before the union, but the NHLPA is concerned about helping their older alumni, especially guys like you, sir, who are . . . financially disadvantaged."

"What's that mean?" he asked.

"It means that you don't have any money," I said.

Scooter laughed. "Well, you're right about that."

"Not anymore," Colby said. "I met with a team from the Players' Association, and we feel that you're entitled to compensation. You've never taken any money from the PA and you played in the NHL for ten seasons. We want to give you"— he paused to check some papers that he held on his lap—"two hundred dollars a month for the 1970s, three hundred dollars a month for the 1980s, four hundred for the 1990s, and five hundred for the 2000s."

Mom gasped and leaned over and hugged Scooter. "This is wonderful!" she squealed.

"Scooter!" I said. "You're rich."

"How rich?" he asked.

"Actually," Colby said, "I have the figure here. Mr. Murphy, you are entitled to one hundred and sixty-eight thousand dollars."

CHAPTER TWENTY-SEVEN

Two days after Scooter's money arrived from the NHLPA, we helped him move into Whispering Pines. Sam came to help us, and Scooter charmed her by saying she was even more beautiful than I'd said she was. I could have died, but Sam seemed really pleased. Scooter had his own room, and he quickly made friends with the men in the pool room and Edna and Phyllis, the euchre players. He liked the bright sunny reading room and spent a lot of time there, trying to teach himself how to read better. It wasn't always easy getting used to this new life. Sometimes he grumbled about having to live by the home's rules, eating dinner at a certain time and all that, but he adjusted pretty quickly—except for one thing.

Whenever the dining hall had doughnuts, he would stuff two or three extra into his pockets when he thought no one was watching. The lady in charge phoned home and asked me if I could please explain to Scooter that he could have as many doughnuts as he wanted, and he didn't need to hide them. I said I would do my best, but if they served old-fashioned glazed then there was nothing I could do.

I started bringing him books from the school library, early readers like Dr. Seuss. His favourite was a book about Maurice "The Rocket" Richard called *The Hockey Sweater*.

"Did you know I blocked his shot in the Stanley Cup final?" he asked, as he studied the pictures in the story.

"Yeah, I know, and Bill Barilko scored the Cup winner on the next shift. Hey, that reminds me, Coach Madigan still owes me a Coke."

"Why's that?" Scooter asked.

"He bet me that you assisted on Barilko's goal."

Scooter smiled slyly. "Next time you make a bet about me, make sure it involves an old-fashioned glazed."

I was listening to Scooter read from *The Hockey Sweater*. He was improving every day, and I rarely had to help him sound out words anymore. But my mind kept wandering. Tomorrow morning I would be leaving to compete in the Quebec Peewee Tournament. I was really excited and a little bit nervous, but I was also feeling something else.

Scooter placed the book in his lap.

"Jake? Nervous about tomorrow?" he asked.

"Not really. It's just that . . . I don't know. Mom's not going to be there."

"Why not?" he asked.

"Can't afford the time off work. I'm staying with Freddie and his parents."

"That will be fun, won't it?" He was obviously trying to cheer me up.

"Yeah, the Talbots are great. It's just that Mom's never missed a game. I guess I just wanted her to come."

I stood and straightened my chair. "I better get going, Scooter."

Scooter got up and held out his hand. I shook it and tried to smile.

"Have a great time," he said.

"Thanks. I'll call you when I get back."

CHAPTER TWENTY-EIGHT

The buzzer sounded in the Quebec Coliseum to end a spirited first period that saw us tied at one goal each with the Boston Junior Bruins. We had more individual skill, but the Bruins were really fast skaters. We spent most of the first period scrambling in our own end. Boston outshot us 12–4, but Freddie was spectacular. Our only goal came on a broken play when two Boston defencemen got their signals crossed and turned the puck over to Lyle Richmond. Lyle dashed in on an unexpected breakaway, made a beautiful deke, and slid the puck past the helpless Boston goaltender. Now we were gathered at the bench for a quick breather. Coach Madigan called for our attention.

"Not bad, boys, not bad," he said. "We were definitely outshot, but Freddie held us in. Now that you've got your first period nerves out of your system, maybe we can calm down a little and play some hockey. What do you think we need to do to improve?"

Sheldon Neely, our best defenceman, piped up. "Everything has to be done quicker," he said.

Lyle agreed. "Yeah. Man, are they quick."

"Okay," Madigan said. "Let's try to get the puck up the boards to our wingers and we'll have the wingers chip the puck out off the boards and into the neutral zone. But do it fast."

There was a general murmur of consent from the team as the referee blew his whistle to start the second period.

Lyle, Joey, and I sat down at the front of the bench. Madigan leaned over my shoulder.

"How you feeling?" he asked.

"I'm okay."

"You seem kind of sluggish," he said.

"They're just real fast, I guess."

"No faster than you, Jakey. Come on, what's bugging you?"

"Nothing, Coach."

"Okay, then, snap out of it and start playing," he challenged.

The second period continued at a frenetic pace. Boston continued to swarm in our end, and we did our best to clear the puck out of our zone and muster an attack of our own. Boston threw ten more shots at Freddie, beating him once, and at the end of the second period, they led 2–1. I worked hard, but I just couldn't seem to get anything going. I was getting tired and frustrated.

As Madigan talked to us in an effort to spark a third-period comeback, I looked around the Coliseum. The former home of the Quebec Nordiques was huge. It was the biggest arena that I had ever played in. In a lot of ways, it was not unlike Maple Leaf Gardens. The Coliseum was, for the most part-empty. Directly across the ice sat a small cluster of parents from Boston.

I scanned to the right and looked over at our cheering section. They didn't look any different than they did at any other game. The dads sat in a row and stared silently at the ice. The moms sat in the row in front of the dads and seemed to be chatting away happily. If they were nervous, they sure weren't showing it.

I was just about to focus my attention back on Coach Madigan when something caught my eye on the far side of the rink. Two people were standing in the tunnel that led to the section of seats where the North York parents were sitting. One of them was wearing a bright red coat.

I know that parka, I thought as a grin spread across my face. And the other coat was a mustard yellow, like my mother's.

As the third period got underway, Madigan leaned in once again. He pointed across the ice.

"Your mom's here," he said.

"I know, I saw her come in with Scooter," I replied.

"Now, start playing," he said.

Boston fired another shot at our net. Freddie snared it with his glove and held it for a whistle. I took the ice for my first shift of the third period feeling refreshed and energized. I won the faceoff back to Sheldon and we quickly broke out of our zone. For the rest of the shift, we buzzed around in Boston's end and established our first really legitimate offence.

The game continued to flow back and forth, but unlike in the first two periods, now we generated as many scoring chances as Boston did. Late in the third period, Boston dumped the puck in on Freddie. He stopped it and then steered it to the side of his net and left it for Sheldon, who grabbed it and circled behind the net. Two Boston forecheckers converged on him and he slid a nice pass between them that ended up right on Lyle's stick. The Boston defenceman should have retreated to the neutral zone, but instead, he attacked toward Lyle. Lyle waited patiently for him to over-commit and then he simply banked the puck off the boards and around the defenceman.

The puck careened out into the neutral zone where I picked it up at full speed. I looked to my right and saw Joey skating as hard as he could up the right side toward the last Boston defenceman. I skated the puck as wide as I could down the left side. When I got to the blue line, I pulled the puck back behind me so that I could shoot or slide a pass to Joey.

The Boston defenceman threw his feet toward his goal and dove onto his chest in what looked like a reverse bellyflop. He slid backwards in an attempt to cut off my ability to make a pass across the ice.

I looked up and could see that the goaltender had come way out of his net to challenge me. I couldn't even see the net, which had all but disappeared behind a wall of goalie equipment. I tried the only play I thought I had left, flicking a delicate pass that arced beautifully through the air and floated just over the outstretched body of the sliding defenceman. The puck landed softly on the ice and slid toward Joey's stick. He had an easy redirect into the wide-open net.

Our bench erupted in celebration as Joey and I collided behind the Boston net in a congratulatory hug.

"Atta boy, Joey!" I yelled.

"Jake, what a pass!" he yelled back.

"Thanks. Now let's go and finish these guys off."

We continued to press, but we were unable to take the

lead, and when the final seconds ticked down we were still tied. Madigan paced back and forth on the bench and tried his best to settle us down. He looked relatively calm himself, except for the fact that his hands were flapping like bird wings.

"Calm down, calm down," he pleaded.

I wondered whether he was talking to himself or the team.

"Listen up, boys," he said. "We've got a five-minute overtime followed by a shootout. Now Freddie has been fantastic, and I think that we'd win a shootout, but let's not take any chances. Jake, let's start your line."

We grabbed one last drink of water, and then the three of us headed out to centre ice.

"You know Coach wants us to score on this shift right?" Lyle said.

"I know," I answered.

"Well, what are we waiting for?" Joey asked.

I was ready to take the faceoff when the referee blew his whistle to start the overtime. I won the draw back to Sheldon, but at the last second the puck took a funny hop and bounced right over Sheldon's stick. He turned and scrambled after it but Boston's left winger was hot on his tail. Sheldon tried to circle behind the net, but the Boston forward was a faster skater. As he went behind the net, the Boston winger hammered Sheldon into the boards and stole the puck from him. He quickly circled back and slid the puck to his defenceman who was set up just inside the blue line. He wound up and pounded a slapshot at the goal.

Freddie made a terrific save, but the puck bounced off to his left. I watched in horror as it landed perfectly on the stick of the Boston centreman.

No! a voice in the back of my head screamed. *Move Jake. Now!*

Just as the kid fired the puck, and I could see him beginning to raise his stick in celebration, I threw myself into the crease. Sliding on my knees, I grimaced as I braced myself for the shot. The puck hit me square in the chest and bounced wildly into the corner of the rink.

Ahhhgggh! Pain knifed through my body. *Man, I hate blocking shots!*

Lyle grabbed the puck in the left corner and looked up just in time to see Boston's right winger bearing down hard on him. He slid the puck through his feet and stepped neatly around him. Lyle took two quick strides and then saw Joey bolting up the right side. Lyle blasted a hard pass over to Joey, who took the puck at full speed and burst through the neutral zone.

Get up! Move! Skate! Now!

I forced myself to my feet and skated up the ice as fast as I could. My chest was killing me, and I was having trouble breathing. I watched as Joey wound up and fired a slapshot. Boston's goalie deflected the shot up the right wall and the puck would have bounced out into the neutral zone, except that Lyle lunged for it and kept the play just onside. He threw the puck back toward their net. Again, the Boston goalie made the save, but the puck got tied up between Joey and a Boston defenceman. The Boston player was able to get his stick on the puck and he shot it toward the blue line.

This time it was Sheldon who managed to hold the Boston zone. As he wound up to unload a slapshot, I finally entered the zone.

"Shelly!" I screamed.

Sheldon hesitated, and I knew instantly that he had heard me. He deked slightly to his right, and I skated as hard as I could toward the left faceoff circle. He wound up for a second time, but instead of shooting, he laced a slap pass across the rink right to where I was standing completely unchecked. I grabbed the pass and instantly released a wrist shot toward the top corner of the net. The Boston goalie was completely fooled by Sheldon's pass and was unable to recover in time. I watched as my shot bulged the back of the twine and then I leaped into the air. A second later I was driven to the ice by Joey, Lyle, Sheldon, and his defence partner, Paul Bradshaw. They were all shouting. The rest of the team piled off the bench and raced to join the celebration. For the second time in the last few minutes I had the wind knocked out of me as I was squished at the bottom of a very loud, very squirmy dog pile, and I knew that there was no place else on earth I would rather be.

After the game, for the first time ever, I changed quickly.

"Why are you in such a rush?" Freddie asked.

"My mom's here."

"I didn't think she was coming."

"Me neither." I grabbed my hockey bag. "Meet you in the lobby."

I found Mom and Scooter standing with the other North York parents. "What are you doing here?" I said as I gave Mom a hug.

"I'll let Scooter tell you," Mom said.

I turned and looked at my friend. "Hi, Scooter."

"Guess what, Jake?" Scooter said.

"What?"

"I went on an airplane!"

"You did? When?"

"Just now, your mom and I flew from Toronto," he said happily.

I looked back at Mom, hoping that she could finally fill in the blanks.

Mom said, "Scooter phoned me the other night to say you were sad that I wasn't coming to Quebec. He said he'd pay for the plane tickets if I could get the time off work and, well, here we are!"

"That's awesome," I said.

"Hey, Jake. I liked your shot block," Scooter said.

I laughed. "Me too. Hey, did it remind you of anyone? 1951? Stanley Cup Final? Murphy's blocked shot on 'The Rocket' allows Leafs to win?"

Scooter guffawed. "I liked yours better," he said.

Suddenly I remembered something. I reached into my pocket and pulled out the puck that I had scored the winning goal with. "Here, Scooter," I said. "I got you the game puck."

Scooter handled it like it was a precious jewel. "Thanks, Jake." He studied the crest on the puck and tried to read it. After a moment, he looked up, defeated. "Jake, I've been working real hard on my reading, but I'm having trouble with this puck."

"That's okay, Scooter," I said slyly. "The puck's written in French. It says *Tournoi International de Hockey Peewee de Québec.*"

"Oh!" Scooter said, clearly impressed by my French. "What's it mean?"

"It means," I said, "that I'm really glad that you two are here."

CHAPTER TWENTY-NINE

We arrived home from Quebec late on Friday night. We ended up going two and two and I had five goals and four assists. We lost in the quarter final to the eventual tournament champs from Sweden. We didn't have any hockey today, but I sure didn't have any time to relax. It had been a whirlwind of haircuts and clothes shopping. Now, as I stood in front of my mirror, I made one final attempt at tying my tie, but gave up in exasperation.

"Mom!" I yelled. "Can you help me?"

Mom opened her door. "Let's have a look at you."

I turned around. She was wearing a beautiful blue dress and her hair was done in a fancy up-do.

"Wow, Mom," I said. "You look really nice."

"Why thank you, Jake," she said. "You don't look so bad yourself. Now let's get this tie done. The limo will be here any second."

Two short months ago, I had been living as a homeless person on the streets of Toronto. Now, tonight, I would be travelling by limousine to attend my first ever Leafs game.

"You ever been in a limo before, Mom?" I asked.

Mom straightened my tie and looked like she was resisting the urge to fuss with my hair. "A few times."

"What are they like?"

Just then the doorbell rang. "Why don't you go see for yourself?"

The limo driver was a big, friendly guy named Lenny. By the time he pulled up at Sam's house, he knew all about Scooter and me and almost seemed like one of the family. He eased the limo up to the curb, got out and opened the door for me.

"Good luck," he whispered, as if he could tell I was nervous.

I walked to the same door I had knocked on hundreds of times over the years, and smoothed my suit with my hands. Sam's dad opened it before I even knocked.

"Well, Jake, you look great," he said.

"Thanks, Mr. Beckett."

"You sure you don't have one more ticket?" he teased.

I relaxed a bit. "Sorry, sir."

I looked up, and there stood Sam at the top of the stairs. She was wearing a purple dress and the first pair of heels I'd ever see her in. She had told me on the phone that she desperately hoped she would make it through the night without tripping.

"Hi, Sam." I couldn't take my eyes off her. She looked absolutely beautiful. "You look really, um . . . really nice."

Sam smiled and got all the way down the stairs without face-planting.

Scooter was waiting outside as the limo pulled up in front of the Whispering Pines Retirement Home. He was wearing a new black suit.

Lenny opened the door, and Scooter eased his way into the limo. "Wow," he said. "It's all a little much, isn't it?"

"You okay, Scooter?" I asked.

He rubbed his hands together briskly. "I'm all right, Jake. I guess I'm just a little edgy."

I knew just how he felt. "Well, we'll get through this together, okay?"

He nodded. "Okay, Jake."

We stood on the red carpet, near the penalty box at the Air Canada Centre, and waited anxiously. I looked around at the arena and marvelled at its size. It was filled to capacity and buzzed with energy as nineteen thousand fans waited to see their beloved Leafs take on the Washington Capitals. Suddenly, the lights in the arena dimmed, and a series of giant Leafs logos was illuminated and began to flash across the ice. The Capitals skated out onto the ice and were immediately met by a chorus of boos from the Leafs fans.

Then the rich, deep voice of the Leafs announcer boomed over the PA system.

"*Ladies and Gentlemen: Here are your Toronto Maple Leafs!*"

The crowd cheered madly as the Leafs dashed onto the ice. After a quick warm-up skate, the two teams gathered at their blue lines.

As the announcer began to speak, a series of images played across the giant LCD screen at centre ice.

"Ladies and Gentlemen: The Toronto Maple Leafs have a rich tradition of excellence which dates back to the early part of the 1900s. Tonight we are pleased to honour one of the greats from years past, who is here tonight to drop the ceremonial first puck.

"In 1951, your Toronto Maple Leafs defeated the Montreal Canadiens to win the Stanley Cup."

The crowd immediately erupted in a large cheer and a chant of "Go Leafs Go" echoed throughout the arena.

"During the overtime of the last game of that series," the announcer continued, *"the great Rocket Richard found himself with an open net. Before he could score, and give the Habs the victory, one of our Leafs heroes dove in front of the Rocket's blast and blocked the shot."*

I looked up at the screen and watched old black-and-white footage of Scooter sprawling in front of the Leafs' empty net.

"You all know what happened next."

The video screen showed Bill Barilko scoring his famous overtime goal, to give the Leafs the victory. As the puck went into the top corner of the net, the crowd erupted and cheered as if they were watching the game live.

"Tonight," the announcer said, *"we have in the building the very man who blocked that shot. He's been away for a long time, but at long last, he's returned home."*

The houselights came up and an usher motioned for us to follow him to centre ice.

"Ladies and Gentlemen: please direct your attention to centre ice.

"*Accompanied by his family, Rebecca and Jake Dumont, and Samantha Beckett, would you please welcome to the Air Canada Centre, the Toronto Maple Leafs' most famous shot blocker—Scooter Murphy.*"

Nineteen thousand people stood in what was not only an enthusiastic ovation, but an amazing welcome home.

As the chants of "Go Leafs Go" echoed around the building, Scooter waved to the crowd. The captains of the two teams skated out to centre ice and prepared to face off in front of Scooter. His hand was shaking ever so slightly as he held the puck.

Suddenly, he turned and looked over at us. His eyes were twinkling with happiness.

"Come here," he said.

I started. "Me?"

"Of course, you. You too, Sam, Rebecca."

Together, the three of us walked over and stood beside him.

"That's better," he said.

I put my hand on his shoulder and watched as Scooter waved one more time to the crowd and then leaned toward the two players and dropped the puck.

AUTHOR'S NOTE

The Toronto Maple Leafs played their last game at Maple Leaf Gardens on February 13, 1999. Aside from a few television and movie shoots, the building was essentially abandoned for a decade. On November 30, 2011, the building reopened, with a large grocery store and a new, smaller arena that is home to the Ryerson University hockey teams. My story takes place between the years 1999 and 2011 when Maple Leaf Gardens sat as an empty building.

Q&A WITH AUTHOR TOM EARLE

Where did you get the idea for this story?

Around the time I was finishing up *The Hat Trick*, my sister-in-law, Susan Carter, said, "Why don't you write a story about Maple Leaf Gardens?" The novel grew out of that one simple suggestion.

How did you come up with the descriptions of the interior of Maple Leaf Gardens after it was closed?

A funny story. I was in Toronto to talk to my editor about *The Hat Trick*, and after our meeting, I walked from the HarperCollins building on Bloor Street down to the Gardens. Back then, the Gardens was an abandoned, boarded-up building. On this day, however, Wood Street was full of white tractor-trailers, and the back of the arena was wide open. A security guard told me that they were filming a TV show inside. This was my big chance to get inside the building, but despite my best begging and bribery attempts, the guard wouldn't let me in. Discouraged, I walked around to the front of the building and came upon one of the actors sitting outside on Carlton Street, eating his lunch. I told him I was writing a story about the Gardens and wanted to take a quick look inside. He said that I would probably be kicked out, but that I was free to take a chance. So, I opened the door, smiled at another security guard, and said, "How ya doing?"

Then I rushed past him and spent the next half-hour scurrying around, trying to see as much of the building as I could. The scene where Jake marvels to himself about standing on the floor of Maple Leaf Gardens happened to me that day. Unfortunately, it wasn't long before the security guards threw me out. They were really nice about it, though.

How did you come up with the character of Scooter Murphy?
Scooter is based partly on a Leafs legend and partly on a real person. When I was a kid, people used to say that Leafs superstar Harvey "Busher" Jackson ended up as a homeless person after his career in the NHL ended in 1944. I'm not sure if this is true or not, but it always made for a good story. Some of Scooter's quirks and expressions are based on my grandfather, Del Earle. He was an incredible athlete (he made it to the 1928 Olympic trials in the pole vault) and maintained a lifelong love of games and competition—board games, cards, pool, ping-pong, shuffleboard, you name it. If you would play with him, he was happy. If he won, he was happier.

Why did you decide not to reveal a lot of details about how Scooter became homeless?

Scooter is homeless mainly for financial reasons: as he got older, he found it more and more difficult to find work. Does he also have a deep, dark secret, such as addiction or mental illness? I think everyone is entitled to their past, both positive and negative, and that a character with an element of mystery is a good thing. For me, *Star Wars* was ruined when they revealed how Anakin Skywalker turned to the dark side. Darth Vader went from this terrifyingly wonderful character with a mysterious past to a whiny crybaby who kills mini-Jedis! I decided to let readers fill in the blanks for themselves.

As a teacher, have you encountered students who have had similar troubles at home to Jake?

Thankfully, I've never had to deal with a student who was being physically abused at home. I have had to help kids through other stuff though, such as poverty. Lots of kids live in homes where money is tight, and that can be really tough. I've known students whose attendance record becomes perfect in the winter because the school is heated.

Jake runs away when the abuse in his house becomes intolerable. What would you suggest a kid in a similar situation do instead?

I created a violent home for Jake because he needed a reason to run away. I would *never* recommend running away in real life. As a teacher, I know there are adults out there who care about kids and can help. You just have to ask. My advice would be to talk to a trusted adult, such as a teacher or a police officer, or call Kids' Help Phone (1-800-668-6868).

You've written two novels about hockey, *Home Ice Advantage* and *The Hat Trick*. What is it about the game that inspires you?

I'm inspired by the skill and the speed of professional players, and I love that you can play the game your whole life. When you are little, you may dream of becoming a pro. Of course, most players will never get close to junior hockey, or college or university hockey, let alone the NHL. But when you're older, you can go out for your weekly skate with your buddies and take comfort in knowing that you're not the only one who still fantasizes about being in the NHL.

You've coached minor hockey for years. Have you ever encountered a parent like Jake's dad?

Are there jerks in hockey? Absolutely. Have I encountered people like Jake's dad? Yes, but they are in an extremely small minority among the thousands and thousands of people who spend their winters in rinks across the country.

Hockey is the greatest game in the world, and what makes it great is the friendships that you make with your teammates. Some of my own parents' closest friends are people they met at the rink when I was a kid playing minor hockey forty years ago.

Now, the same thing has happened to me. And some of the guys I play hockey with have been teammates of mine since we were kids. That is, quite simply, awesome.